# The Case of the

# Amorous Aunt

## Erle Stanley Gardner

BALLANTINE BOOKS • NEW YORK

Copyright © 1963 by Erle Stanley Gardner

Copyright renewed 1991 by Jean Bethell Gardner and Grace Naso

All rights reserved under International and Pan-American Copyright Conventions. Published in the United States of America by Ballantine Books, a division of Random House, Inc., New York, and simultaneously in Canada by Random House of Canada Limited, Toronto.

Library of Congress Catalog Card Number: 63-8803

ISBN 0-345-37878-4

This edition published by arrangement with William Morrow and Company

Printed in Canada

First Ballantine Books Edition: April 1994

10  9  8  7  6  5  4  3  2  1

# Foreword

The archenemy of the murderer is the autopsy.

In crimes of emotion the autopsy can determine facts that no subsequent fabrication, however clever, can confute.

In cold-blooded crimes committed by an intellectual and scheming murderer who has greed or revenge as his goal, the medical examiner, following clues which would never be apparent to a less thoroughly trained individual, can establish the truth.

It is for this reason that I have, in these Perry Mason books, tried to interest the reader in the vital importance of legal medicine.

Legal medicine is, of course, international in scope. In Mexico City, for instance, the number of official autopsies performed is approximately equal to those performed in New York City.

My friend Dr. Manuel Merino Alcántara is Sub-Director of the Mexican Forensic Institute, Professor of Legal Medicine at the National University of Mexico Medical School, and editor of *El Medico*, the Mexican medical journal, similar in scope to the American Medical Association's *Journal* in this country. He is diligently working to bring about international co-operation and understanding in the field of legal medicine, and has sent me a great deal of statistical information.

And so I dedicate this book to Mexico's outstanding authority in forensic medicine,

### DR. MANUEL MERINO ALCÁNTARA

ERLE STANLEY GARDNER

# Chapter 1

Della Street, Perry Mason's confidential secretary, said, "A couple of lovebirds have strayed into the office without an appointment. They insist it's a matter of life and death."

"Everything is," Mason said. "If you start with the idea of perpetuating life, you must accept the inevitable corollary of death—but I presume these people aren't interested in my philosophical ideas."

"These people," Della Street announced, "are interested in each other, in the singing of the birds, the blue of the sky, the moonlight on water, the sound of the night wind in the trees."

Mason laughed. "It's infectious. You are getting positively romantic, poetic, and show evidence of having been exposed to a highly contagious disease. . . . Now, what the devil would two lovebirds want with the services of a lawyer who specializes in murder cases?"

Della Street smiled enigmatically. "I told them that I thought you'd see them, despite the fact they have no appointment."

"In other words," the lawyer said, "your own curiosity having been aroused, you decided to arouse mine. Did they tell you what they wanted to see me about?"

"A widowed aunt," Della Street said, "and a Bluebeard."

Mason made an elaborate show of rubbing his hands together.

"Sold!" he exclaimed.

"Now?" Della Street asked.

"Immediately," Mason said. "When's the next appointment, Della?"

"Fifteen minutes, but you can keep him waiting for a

few minutes. He's the witness in that Dowling affair, the one that Paul Drake located."

Mason frowned. "I don't want to take any chances on having *him* leave the office. Let me know the minute he comes in, Della, and send in the lovebirds. What are their names?"

Della Street consulted a memo.

"George Latty and Linda Calhoun. They're from some little town in Massachusetts. It's their first trip to California."

"Bring them in," Mason said.

Della Street went to the reception room, to return in a matter of seconds with the young couple.

Mason sized them up as he rose and smiled a greeting.

The man was twenty-three or twenty-four; tall, rather handsome, with two-inch sideburns and wavy black hair that had been carefully groomed.

The young woman was certainly not more than twenty-two, with round blue eyes which she held wide open in such a way as to give her face an expression of almost cherubic innocence.

As they stood surveying Mason, the girl's hand unconsciously groped for and found the hand of her escort, and they stood there hand in hand, the girl smiling, the man self-conscious.

"You're George Latty," Mason said to the man.

He nodded.

"And you're Miss Linda Calhoun."

The girl nodded.

"Sit down, please," Mason said, "and tell me what seems to be the trouble."

They seated themselves, and Linda Calhoun looked at George Latty as though signaling him to break the ice. Latty, however, sat looking straight ahead.

"Well?" Mason asked.

"You tell him, George," the girl said.

Latty leaned forward and put his hands on the lawyer's desk. "It's her aunt," he said.

2

"And what about the aunt?" Mason asked.

"She's going to get murdered."

"Have you any idea who is going to commit the murder?" Mason asked.

"Certainly," Latty said. "His name is Montrose Dewitt."

"And what," Mason asked, "do you know about Montrose Dewitt, aside from the fact that he's a potential murderer?"

It was Linda Calhoun who answered the question.

"Nothing," she said. "That's why we're here."

"Now, you folks are from Massachusetts, I believe?"

"That's right," Latty said.

"You've known each other for some time?"

"Yes."

"If it's not a personal question, may I ask if you're engaged?"

"Yes, we are."

Mason said, "Forgive me if I seem to be impertinent, but if we're going to get into a case of this sort where there may be some name calling, I want to be sure of my facts. Has the date been set for the wedding?"

"No," she said. "George is studying law and I'm ..." She flushed. "I'm helping him through law school."

"I see," Mason said. "You're employed?"

"Yes."

Mason raised his eyebrows in silent interrogation.

"I'm a secretary in a law firm," she said. "I applied for and received a month's leave of absence and came out here. Before I left, I asked the senior partner for the name of the best attorney in this part of the country and he said that I should consult you if it came to a knock-down, drag-out fight."

"And it has come to a knock-down, drag-out fight?" Mason asked.

"It's going to."

Mason looked at Latty. "Now," he said, "as I take it, you young people came on here together. May I ask if you drove, came by plane or—"

3

"I drove," she said. "That is, I came with Aunt Lorraine, and George came out by plane when I ... when I telephoned him."

"And when was that?"

"Last night. He just got in this morning and we had a council of war and decided to come to you."

"All right," Mason said, "that gives us the preliminaries. Now tell me about Aunt Lorraine. What's her last name?"

"Elmore. E-l-m-o-r-e."

"Miss or Mrs?"

"Mrs. She's a widow. And she's ... well, she's at the foolish age."

"And exactly what age is considered the foolish age?"

"She'll be forty-eight on her next birthday."

"And what has she done that indicates her foolishness?"

"She's gone overboard," Latty said.

Mason raised his eyebrows.

"In love," the young woman explained.

Mason smiled. "I take it that people around twenty-one and twenty-two who are in love are perfectly normal, but they're supposed to have a corner on the emotion and anyone above that age who falls in love is indulging in foolishness?"

Linda flushed.

"Well, at that age," Latty said, "well ... sure."

Mason laughed. "You two have all the arrogance of youth. Perhaps the best thing one can say for youth is that it's not incurable. Your aunt's husband died, Miss Calhoun?"

"Yes."

"How long ago?"

"About five years ago. And please don't laugh at us, Mr. Mason. This is serious."

Mason said, "I would say your aunt had every right in the world to fall in love."

"But it's the way she did it," Linda protested.

Latty said, "Some adventurer is going to strip her of all of her money."

Mason's eyes narrowed. "Are you the only relative?" he asked Linda.

"Yes."

"And presumably you were the sole beneficiary under her will?"

The girl flushed again.

Mason waited for her answer.

"Yes, I suppose so."

"Is she wealthy?"

"She has . . . well, rather a comfortable nest egg."

"And within the last few weeks," Latty said, "her entire attitude has changed. She used to be very affectionate with Linda and now her affections have been alienated by this cad. Yesterday there was a fight and Lorraine walked out on Linda and told her to go back to Massachusetts and quit messing up her life."

Mason said, "And just what is your interest in the matter, Mr. Latty?"

"Well, I . . . I'm—"

"You're in love with Linda and expect to marry her?"

"Yes."

"And perhaps you had been rather counting on Aunt Lorraine's nest egg coming in at some time in the future?"

"Absolutely not!" he said. "I resent that."

"I was asking you," Mason said, "because if we take any action other people will ask you that question, and perhaps in a sneering tone of voice. I thought I'd prepare you, that's all."

Latty said, "Let them make that accusation to my face and I'll flatten them."

Mason said, "You'll do a lot better to keep your temper, young man. Now, Miss Calhoun, I'd like to hear the facts of the case. Can you begin at the beginning and tell me when this first came up?"

She said, "Aunt Lorraine has been lonely. I know that, and I sympathize with her. I'm the only one she has and I've done what I could."

"Doesn't she have friends?" Mason asked.

"Well, yes, but not . . . well, not what you'd call intimate friends."

"But you've been in touch with her?"

"I've given her every minute of my time that I could, Mr. Mason, but— Well, I'm a working girl. I have to keep up my apartment and I have a job to do. I know that Aunt Lorraine would like to have seen more of me and—"

"And you put in a good deal of your time seeing something of George Latty?" Mason asked.

"Yes."

"And your aunt, perhaps, resented that?"

"I think she resented him."

"All right. Now, what happened with this Montrose Dewitt?"

"She met him by correspondence."

"One of those lonely heart things?" Mason asked.

"Heavens, no! She isn't *that* foolish. It was some kind of a deal where Aunt Lorraine wrote to a magazine expressing an opinion on one of the articles that the magazine had published, and the magazine published the letter with her name and not her street address but the city where she lived.

"Mr. Dewitt sent her a letter just addressed to her at that city, and the post office located her address and delivered the letter, and that started a correspondence."

"And then?" Mason asked.

"Then Aunt Lorraine became very much smitten. She wouldn't admit it, of course, not even to herself, but I could see it.

"She sent him her picture and, incidentally, it was a picture that was taken some ten years ago."

"Did he send her his picture?"

"No. He told her that he wore a patch over one eye and was very self-conscious about it."

"And then?" Mason asked.

"Then he called her long distance and after that he would call her quite frequently, two or three times a week.

"So of course Aunt Lorraine insisted she was going to

take a vacation; a long motor trip. Well, that didn't fool me any, and I knew what she had in mind, but there was nothing anyone could do about it. You couldn't stop her at that time. Things had gone too far, and the man had her completely hypnotized."

"So you decided to go with her."

"Yes."

"And you came out here with her and then what happened?"

"We checked in at a hotel and she said she was going to lie down for a while. I went out to do some shopping. When I came back she was gone. There was a note on the dresser for me, saying she might not be back until late.

"When she came in I accused her of having gone out to see Montrose Dewitt and she became angry and said she didn't care to be chaperoned, nor did she care to have me treat her as though she were in her second childhood."

"Her feelings were quite understandable," Mason said.

"I know," Linda Calhoun said, "but there are other things, other disturbing factors."

"Such as what?"

"I found out that she had taken the blood tests necessary to obtain a marriage license, that she had been converting a great deal of property to cash. She had been selling some of her stocks and bonds, and she came out here with something like thirty-five thousand dollars in cash."

"No traveler's checks?"

"Just cold, hard cash, Mr. Mason. A roll of bills that would—I believe the expression they customarily use is, choke a horse."

"And what caused her to do that?"

"Your guess is as good as mine," she said, "but I don't think there's any question but that it was an action prompted by instructions she had received from Montrose Dewitt over the telephone."

"This Dewitt seems to be rather a vague and shadowy character," Mason said. "What has she told you about his background?"

"Nothing. Absolutely nothing. She has been very mysterious about it."

"So you had an argument last night?"

"No, that was yesterday. The night she went out was night before last. Then yesterday she told me she was going to be gone all day and I could be free to do whatever I wanted to, and then I started talking to her and I guess that was the first time I let her know that I knew anything about the money."

"And?" Mason asked.

"And she became absolutely furious. She told me that she had thought I cared for her for herself but that now she was convinced that I cared for her only for what I thought I could get out of her . . . that— Well, she said some things about George that I simply couldn't take."

"Such as what?" Mason asked.

"I don't like to repeat them."

"Does George know?"

"I know," George said. "That is, I know generally."

"He doesn't know *all*," Linda Calhoun said.

"She said that he was a sponge and a heel?" Mason asked.

"That was the start of it," she said. "She went on from there and amplified. She said that if it came to a question of talking about boy friends, at least *her* boy friend was self-supporting and was a *man*, and had some ability to take care of himself in the world without hiding behind a woman's skirts. She—"

"Oh, Mr. Mason, I'm not going to tell you *all* of it. You can use your imagination and—"

"So your aunt told you to go back home?"

"She made it a very humiliating experience. She carefully counted out the money for airplane fare, pointed out that it was first-class fare on a jet plane and told me to take the plane."

"What did you do?"

"I threw the money on the floor, and last night I telephoned George. Then I wired him the money for plane fare."

"Out of your savings?" Mason asked.

"Out of my savings."

"And that's the situation to date?"

"That's all of the situation to date."

Mason said, "Look here, your aunt is a mature woman. If she wants—"

"I know what you're going to say," Linda interrupted, "and I'm not going to interfere with whatever she wants to do. But I do want to find out something about this Montrose Dewitt. I want to protect her from him and from herself."

"That," Mason said, "is going to cost you money . . . more from your savings."

"How much more?"

"A really good private detective agency would want around fifty dollars a day and expenses."

"How many days would it take?"

"Heaven knows," Mason said. "A detective might get all the information he needed in a few hours. He might get it in a day. He might have to work for a week or a month."

"I can't afford to have him for a month," she said, "but I could— Well, I thought that if I could pay two hundred dollars—but of course there'd be *your* fee."

"You don't need me," Mason said. "There's nothing connected with the case that has any legal angles. You don't contend that your aunt is unable to manage her own affairs, that she's mentally unsound?"

"Certainly not. She's simply at a dangerous age and she's in love."

Mason smiled and said, "Whenever a person falls in love it's automatically a dangerous age. Now, do I understand you want to engage a private detective?"

"Yes. And if you could see that we didn't go wrong— Well, I understand there are some private detectives who— Well, some are better than others."

"And you want the best. Is that it?"

"Yes."

Mason nodded to Della Street. "Ring the Drake Detective Agency and ask Paul Drake to step in, if you will please, Della."

Mason turned to his visitors. "Paul Drake," he said, "has his offices on this floor. The Drake Detective Agency does all of my business and has for years, and you'll find Paul Drake exceedingly competent and completely honest."

A few moments later when Drake's code knock sounded on the door, Della Street let him in and Mason performed the introductions.

Paul Drake, tall, loose-jointed, surveyed the young couple with shrewd eyes, and seated himself.

Mason said, "I'll make it short, Paul. Linda Calhoun and George Latty are engaged. Linda has an aunt, Lorraine Elmore, forty-seven, a widow. Mrs. Elmore engaged in correspondence with a man by the name of Montrose Dewitt and seems to have fallen pretty much under his influence. She has had blood tests taken, apparently to get a marriage license. Linda and her aunt came out here on a vacation. Her aunt is carrying perhaps as much as thirty-five thousand in cash. She and Linda had a fight. Mrs. Elmore told Linda to go home. Instead of that, Linda wired money to George Latty and had him fly out to join her. They want to save her aunt from herself. Their home is Massachusetts.

"Particularly, they want to find out all the background on Montrose Dewitt. What will it cost?"

"I don't know," Drake said. "My rates are fifty dollars a day." He turned to Linda Calhoun. "You have his address?"

"Yes. He lives in the Bella Vista Apartments in Van Nuys."

"Photograph?"

"No."

Drake said, "I don't want to take any of your money unless it's a matter of sufficient importance to let me feel I'm not robbing you."

"Do you consider murder a matter of importance, Mr. Drake?"

The detective smiled. "Yes," he said.

"That's what I'm worried about," Linda Calhoun said. "I want to prevent a murder."

Drake said, "I gather you've been reading some of the so-called true crime magazines."

"I have," she stated, "and I'm proud of it! I think every law-abiding citizen should realize the crime hazards of civilized life. One of the big troubles with the administration of justice is that the average citizen doesn't have any idea of the menace of crime."

"You have a point there," Drake agreed, studying her thoughtfully.

"Don't you think it's a suspicious circumstance that Aunt Lorraine is carrying over thirty thousand dollars in cash with her?"

"I think that is more apt to indicate foolishness or falling in love."

"Falling in love with a complete stranger," Linda pointed out.

"All right," Drake said smiling. "You win. Do you want me to go to work on this Montrose Dewitt?"

"I wish you would. At least for . . . well, shall we say, two days?"

"Two days it is," Drake said.

She turned to Mason. "Do you think I should notify the police?"

"Heavens, no!" Mason exclaimed. "That way you really would stir up a hornet's nest. But I do think it's a good idea to have Paul Drake give the situation a once-over. . . . And now, if you'll pardon me, I have an important appointment."

"How much do we owe you, Mr. Mason?"

Mason grinned. "Nothing, as yet. But keep in touch with me and I'll keep in touch with Paul Drake. He'll report to you."

Drake said, "You two had better come down to my office and give me all the data you have. I'll want some background on your aunt and I want everything you know about Montrose Dewitt."

# Chapter 2

Shortly before noon Della Street, answering the telephone, turned to Mason and said, "There's another development in the Case of the Amorous Aunt."

Mason raised his eyebrows in silent interrogation.

"A man named Howland Brent would like to see you at once upon a matter of the greatest importance connected with the affairs of Lorraine Elmore."

"How did he happen to come to me?" Mason asked.

"Apparently Linda Calhoun told him you were representing her."

Mason frowned. "I told her she didn't need an attorney. I did this so she could take what money she had to spend and hire the Drake Detective Agency."

"Well?" Della Street asked. "Do we refer him to Paul Drake or . . ."

Mason looked at his watch. "I have about fifteen minutes before I have to leave for my luncheon appointment, Della. Go take a look at him. If it's routine, refer him to Paul Drake. If it impresses you as being something worth while, come back and let me know and I'll give him fifteen minutes."

Della Street nodded, slipped through the door to the outer office, was gone about five minutes, then returned and said, "I think you'd better see him, Chief."

"How come?" Mason asked.

"He's flown out here from Boston. He's Lorraine Elmore's financial manager. He has charge of all of her investments and he's worried."

"How worried?"

"Plenty. He flew out here."

Mason frowned. "Everyone else regards this situation as being more serious than I do. What does he look like, Della?"

Della Street said slowly, "Let's see. He's somewhere in his late forties, a tall, cadaverous individual with narrow shoulders, a thin waist, high cheekbones, sunken cheeks, a little mustache and one of those little hats the Easterners wear with about an inch and a half brim. He's wearing a tweed suit, rather heavy-soled walking shoes, and carries a cane."

"In short," Mason said, grinning, "he looks like you expected him to look."

Della Street smiled. "And we'll see him?"

"By all means," Mason said. "We'll see him."

Della Street left the office to return in a few moments with Howland Brent.

"This is Mr. Mason, Mr. Brent," she said.

Brent dropped the crook of his cane over his left arm, strode across to Mason's desk, extended a bony hand.

"Ah, Mr. Mason," he said.

"Sit down," Mason invited. "I only have a moment. My secretary tells me you're interested in a matter concerning Lorraine Elmore?"

"Perhaps I should introduce myself in greater detail," Brent said. "I will, however, explain the circumstances as succinctly as possible."

Mason caught Della Street's eye. "Go ahead."

"Very well. I am a financial consultant and manager. I have several clients who give me complete carte blanche in connection with their financial affairs. I invest their monies and reinvest. Beyond a checking account which they carry in their own names, I relieve them of all financial details. From time to time I make reports, of course.

"As my clients need money, they call on me for whatever amount they need. Every thirty days I mail them a complete statement showing their investments, and, of course, the client has the final power of disposition. If the client wishes me to sell certain securities, I sell. If the client wishes me to buy, I buy.

"However, Mr. Mason, I point with pride to my record. I have, over a period of years, made substantial capital gain increases for my clients. I have a very select clientele—one which is also very limited because in matters of this sort I do not believe in the delegation of authority. I reach my own decisions, although those decisions are of course based upon detailed analyses of the securities market and these analyses are, of course, prepared by experts."

Mason nodded.

"I cannot violate the confidence of a client, Mr. Mason, except in a matter that would be tantamount to life or death. I feel that this matter is of such a nature."

"After talking with Linda Calhoun, I take it," Mason said.

"Yes, after talking with Linda Calhoun; although I may point out, Mr. Mason, that my talk with Linda Calhoun was the result of suspicion on my part and that the suspicion was not engendered by my talk with her. In fact, the reverse is the case."

Mason nodded.

"Because my relation with my clients is so highly confidential and so very intimate, I have powers of attorney from the various people I represent; and from time to time I can, if necessary, secure any information which I need from their financial depositaries.

"In this particular case there are blanket instructions that if the checking account falls below a certain amount, the bank is to notify me and I make a sufficient deposit to keep the minimal balance. A situation of this sort seldom arises, but there have been times when my client was traveling when it has been necessary for me to deposit funds.

"I may say without divulging any confidence that Mrs. Elmore's financial sense is very good but her mathematical sense is somewhat deficient. She frequently makes expenditures without keeping accurate account of the aggregate amount."

Mason nodded.

"So, when Mrs. Elmore advised me that she was driving to the West Coast on a vacation, I simply made a routine notation. I may say, however, that she had shortly before the trip asked me to deposit a very substantial amount of cash in her checking account. While I cannot divulge the exact amount, I will state that I considered it somewhat excessive and pointed out that commercial accounts were barren as far as income-producing returns were concerned and that there would be an inevitable loss of interest. However, I was instructed not to bother myself about that but simply to see that sufficient securities were sold so that the funds could be placed in the checking account.

"You follow me, Mr. Mason?"

"One might say I'm a paragraph ahead of you," Mason said. "I take it Mrs. Elmore gave some checks which resulted in the bank's balance falling below the minimum amount; the bank notified you; you were astounded; you used your power of attorney to check with the bank and found out Mrs. Elmore had withdrawn a huge sum in the form of cash."

Brent's expression showed surprise. "That is a remarkable deduction, Mr. Mason."

"It is accurate?"

"It is accurate."

"And why do you come to me?"

"I came out here to consult Mrs. Elmore. I arrived at the airport about two hours ago. I called at the hotel where she was stopping. I found that she had left, that her niece, Miss Calhoun was there; and, while I did not of course confide in Miss Calhoun, I let her know that I was there upon a matter of some urgency and Miss Calhoun confided in me."

"About Montrose Dewitt?"

"Exactly."

"And why did you come to me?" Mason asked.

"I wanted you to have certain information which I felt I could disclose—information which you have deduced so that I do not now have to make a disclosure, and this, of course, is exceedingly gratifying to me because I do like to preserve the confidences of my clients.

"However, Mr. Mason, I wish to impress upon you that the situation is, in my opinion, serious and that it should not be discounted. I would like to have you report to me everything that you find out about my client and about Mr. Dewitt."

Mason shook his head.

"No?" Brent asked.

"No," Mason said.

"You mean it is impossible?"

"I mean it is inadvisable," Mason said. "In the first place, I do not actually have a lawyer-client relationship with anyone. I have recommended a reputable detective agency. Your present contact is with Linda Calhoun, and I would suggest that you can best secure the information you want by keeping in touch with her."

Brent arose from his chair, said, "I see," thought for a moment and added, "I appreciate your position, Mr. Mason. You cannot give me information. However, you have the information which I wanted to be certain was in your hands. Thank you, and good morning."

"Good morning," Mason said.

Brent strode in a dignified manner toward the door through which he had entered the office.

Mason said, "You may go out through the exit door here, if you prefer, Mr. Brent."

Brent turned, surveyed the office, unhooked the cane from his left arm, put it in his right hand and made a dignified exit through the door into the corridor.

Just as he stepped into the corridor, he turned, said, "Thank you, Mr. Mason—and Miss Street," put the narrow-rimmed hat on his head and then released the door, letting it gently close behind him.

Mason looked at Della Street and grinned.

She looked at her watch. "You have just sufficient time to make your luncheon appointment," she said.

Mason shook his head. "I'll wait thirty seconds," he said.

"Riding down in the same elevator with Howland Brent might lead to an elevator conversation, and I deplore elevator conversations."

## Chapter 3

It was nearly three that afternoon when Drake's code knock sounded on the hall door of Mason's private office.

Mason nodded to Della Street and she opened the door.

"Thanks, Beautiful," Drake said.

"What's new, Paul?" Mason asked. "Getting anywhere with the Bluebeard?"

Drake looked serious. "There's just a chance, Perry—just a ten-to-one chance—that these people may have something."

"How come?"

"Dewitt had a bank account, something like fifteen thousand dollars. He drew a check which cleaned it out, told the manager of the apartment house where he has an apartment that he might be gone for a month or six weeks, paid two months' rent in advance. He sold his car for cash and took off in an automobile with a rather good-looking woman. They seemed to be very palsy-walsy. The back of the car was loaded with baggage, and the car had a Massachusetts license plate."

"You didn't get the number?"

"Not the number, just the state."

"What did you find about his background?"

"He's been living in this apartment house, the Bella Vista, out in Van Nuys, for about fourteen months. He's rather a dashing type, wears a black eye patch, but has never explained to anyone how he lost the sight of that eye.

"No one seems to know exactly what he does, but it's some kind of a manufacturer's agency deal. He comes and goes on selling trips, keeps pretty much to himself, and apparently has never had a girl friend.

18

"The manager of the apartment sort of worried about that. There are two types of tenants that bother her: those that have too many girl friends and those that don't have any.

"Of course she's supposed to be running a respectable place, and when one of her single tenants has a crush on someone of the opposite sex the manager pretends not to notice, but she notices all right and knows pretty much what's going on.

"When a lone tenant—a bachelor in particular—doesn't have any girl friends, she sizes up the situation with a jaundiced eye because it's abnormal and— Well, you get the picture."

"I get it," Mason said. "You don't know where they went, do you, Paul?"

"Not yet, but I'll find out. I have men working on that angle."

"You say this woman was good-looking, Paul?" Mason asked.

"I gather that she wasn't any chicken," Paul said, "but she was snaky. You can figure it out. Here's a widow who has been lonely for several years. She's too young to be put on the shelf. She meets a man who is interested in her as a woman and starts blossoming out and all of a sudden she's tripping the light fantastic in the romantic environment of a second springtime."

Mason frowningly digested Drake's information.

"So," Drake said, "I just dropped in to tell you that there *may* be something to Linda's suspicions."

"Not Linda's," Mason corrected, smiling. "George's."

"You think he's the one back of it?"

Mason said, "I'll put it this way. I think he triggered the crisis."

"Well," Drake said, "I hated to take Linda's money, but I realized she was going to get some other agency if I didn't get on the job, and I thought I could perhaps clean it up fast, getting some character references on Dewitt and perhaps letting him know he was being investigated.

"You know how it is with a con man, Perry. The minute he thinks that his potential sucker is investigating him he drops that sucker like a hot potato. The one thing those con people can't stand is an investigation."

Mason nodded.

"So," Drake went on, "I had one of my men get into Dewitt's apartment. He was in there for three hours dusting the place for fingerprints, and there wasn't a single fingerprint in the whole apartment."

Mason frowned. "Not a single latent?"

"Not a one."

"But there'd have to be," Mason said. "Good heavens ..."

"Exactly," Drake said as Mason stopped. "It was deliberate. Someone had taken a chamois skin or a treated dust rag and had gone over every place where there would have been a fingerprint; the medicine cabinet in the bathroom; the kitchen faucets; the ice box; the jars inside the ice box—every single place where you'd expect to find a fingerprint had been wiped absolutely clean."

Mason's eyes narrowed.

"So," Drake said, "we then traced the car Dewitt had sold. It's five years old, in pretty good mechanical shape. He got eight hundred and fifty dollars cash from a dealer.

"My man got on the good side of the dealer, got permission to dust the car for fingerprints, telling him that he was looking for the fingerprints of a passenger to whom Dewitt had given a ride.

"There wasn't a single fingerprint in the car."

"Not even on the back of the rearview mirror?" Mason asked.

"Not anywhere on the car; not a single fingerprint. It had been gone over clean. My man made judicious inquiries and found that Dewitt had been wearing gloves when he drove in and sold the car.

"So I got busy on another angle," Drake said. "I traced the history of the car. It had been sold by a used car dealer to Dewitt when he had moved into Van Nuys a little over a year ago."

"What was the idea checking the car?" Mason asked.

"Because there wasn't anything else to check," Drake said, "and I wanted to do a job. I wanted to find out, if I could, something about the guy's background, and I was running down every lead I could get.

"Now, here's a peculiar thing, Perry. Dewitt is away quite a good deal of the time. He's supposed to be traveling on the road. He is supposed to be a manufacturer's agent, but he bought this car thirteen months ago. The used car dealer had his records on the car although it was a job digging up those records. It happens that he keeps careful records on everything because of his guarantee on used cars. The car had gone a little over thirty thousand miles when it was sold to Dewitt, and the car now has thirty-one thousand, eight hundred and seventy-six miles."

Mason frowned.

"In other words," Drake said, "the car has been driven a little over eighteen hundred miles in thirteen months. Now, try and figure that one out."

Mason's eyebrows leveled in frowning concentration. "And yet he's supposed to do a lot of traveling, Paul?"

"Supposed to do a lot of traveling."

"It doesn't add up," Mason said. "Are you sure about the mileage?"

"Just as sure as anyone can be."

"Perhaps the speedometer has been set back, or perhaps a new speedometer was put on."

"In the case of a new speedometer," Drake said, "the mileage would have gone back to zero. In case it had been set back, the question is why, and by whom?"

Mason said, "By Dewitt, in order to make the car look like a better buy when he turned it in."

"It could have been, all right," Drake said. "But I've had a mechanic check the speedometer. There's no sign that it has ever been tampered with, and the mechanic said if it had been tampered with recently, he'd have found evidence."

"I suppose you've traced all the marriage records?" Mason asked.

"Sure. There was a marriage license for a Montrose Dewitt and Belle Freeman taken out a little over two years ago, but the marriage never seems to have taken place.

"I got Miss Freeman's address and telephone number, but my men haven't been able to locate her. No one answers the phone. However, I passed that information on to Linda Calhoun. She said she'd keep trying to get Belle Freeman on the phone.

"Of course, just a marriage license doesn't mean anything. That is, you can't pin a bigamy charge on a person simply on the strength of a marriage license. But my men are working on it and they'll contact her before very long, and Linda will probably reach her. Right at the moment this Freeman girl appears to be our best lead."

Mason reached a sudden decision. "All right, Paul," he said. "Put more men on the job. Get Dewitt located by finding that car with the Massachusetts license number. It shouldn't be too difficult. Put as many men on it as you need and send the bill to me.

"You can bill Linda Calhoun for two days' work at fifty dollars a day, and don't let her know anything about my contributions to the cause.

"I feel I dismissed this matter too lightly and that I may thereby be responsible for any of Aunt Lorraine's future misfortunes. I felt that if it cost Linda a couple of hundred dollars to find out that her aunt was still relatively young and full of romance, it would be a good lesson for her. She'd leave her aunt alone in the future and eventually the affection which had existed between them would be restored. However, I guess we'd better get busy."

"Of course," Drake said, "It *may* be just coincidence, but it is a perfect setup for—"

"Coincidence be damned!" Mason interrupted. "In this

22

business we can't afford to overlook the obvious. We can't afford to overlook anything.

"Get busy, Paul, and try to find out where they are. Put out enough men to cover the motels and—"

"Whoa, back up!" Drake said. "You leave that end of the business to me, Perry. You're going at this thing like an amateur. It would cost a fortune to put out men to cover all the motels and try and trace a big, shiny car with a Massachusetts license number."

"Well, how else *would* you get them?" Mason asked.

Drake grinned. "You have to figure human nature."

The detective turned to Della Street. "What would *you* do if you were in her shoes, Della?"

"Put off my departure long enough to spend some time at a beauty parlor," Della said promptly.

Drake grinned. "There you are, Perry. In a deal of this kind we always try to locate the beauty shop the woman went to. That usually isn't too difficult, and a beauty shop is frequently a gold mine of information. A woman all keyed up with a new romance, bursting with the desire to confide in someone, spending two or three hours in a beauty shop, is certainly going to let the cat out of the bag somehow, somewhere.

"You'd be surprised at what these girls in the beauty shops hear, and you'd also be surprised at how shrewd they are at putting two and two together."

"Okay," Mason said, "cover the beauty shops."

"The one we want is already being covered," Drake said. "It wasn't too difficult to find where she went. I'm waiting for a report which should come in at any minute."

Mason pushed back his swivel chair, got up and started pacing the floor. "What annoys me, Paul, is that I underestimated the potential dangers of the situation. When you come right down to it, I was just a little irritated at George Latty. The guy isn't working his way through law school. He's letting Linda put him through law school, and when she phoned him she'd had a fight with her aunt, instead of telling her, 'Well, Linda, it's your aunt and your business,' he jumps on a plane and spends Linda's money coming out to hold her hand."

"*She* was holding *his* hand," Della Street said, smiling.

The telephone rang.

"That's the unlisted, direct line," Della Street said. "It's probably for you, Paul. Your office has the number."

Drake scooped up the telephone, said, "Hello . . . yes. . . . Yes, this is Paul. What is it?"

Drake listened for a few minutes, said, "Okay, good work. All right, I'll check into it. I'll probably be calling you back. Where are you now?— Okay, stay there until I give you a ring. I'll call you—win, lose or draw."

Drake hung up the phone, said, "Mrs. Elmore talked to the hairdresser. She got started and couldn't stop. She was simply bursting with excitement. They're driving to Yuma to get married. Then they're going to spend their honeymoon at Grand Canyon."

Mason looked at his watch. "You say he withdrew all his balance from the bank, Paul?"

"That's right."

"And paid two months' rent in advance?"

"Yes."

"By check?"

"I don't know. The manager of the apartment house said the rent was paid."

"You talked with her?"

"Yes. I talked with her shortly before noon."

"Friendly?"

"Yes."

Mason gestured toward the phone. "Get her on the line, Paul. Let's see if it was a check. If it was, let's see if it's good. He may have overlooked a bet there."

Drake put through the call to Van Nuys, talked a few minutes, then cupped his hand over the phone, turned to Mason. "She presented the check at the bank an hour ago; the check was turned down, account closed, no funds."

Mason reached a sudden decision.

"Go out there and grab that check, Paul. Get her to let you represent her for collection—"

"She doesn't want to prosecute," Drake interrupted, still holding his palm over the mouthpiece. "She says it's an oversight and he'll make it good."

Mason said, "Damn it, Paul, don't be a sap. Go out there. Get that check. Buy it if you have to. Meet us at the airport. We'll have a chartered plane ready."

He turned to Della Street. "Ring up our plane charter service, Della. Get a twin-motored plane that will take us to Yuma."

Paul Drake said into the phone, "I want to talk with you, Mrs. Ostrander. Will you wait for me, please? I'll be right out."

Della Street reached for the phone as Paul Drake put it down.

"At the airport, Paul," Mason repeated, as the detective headed for the door. "Step on it."

## Chapter 4

The checkerboarded fields of the Imperial Valley were refreshingly green with irrigated crops. Then the highline canal stretched like a huge snake below the plane and immediately the desert took over.

It was as abrupt as that.

Below the highline canal irrigation had turned the desert into a rich, fertile area. On the other side of the canal there was nothing but sand and a long straight ribbon of paved highway.

Mason, looking down on the highway and at the cars that were a mere succession of moving dots, said, "Somewhere down there our quarry is speeding along toward Yuma."

Della Street, her eyes thoughtful, said, "What a situation it is. A woman, at a time of life when affection could mean so much to her, thinking that she has found a perfect mate, hypnotized by her own loyalty, looking through the windshield with starry eyes; while the man driving the car is debating in his mind the details of murder—just when it shall take place so that he can be assured of a safe getaway."

Paul Drake, up in the copilot's seat, looked back and said, "Don't feel too sorry for that woman, Della. Women like her keep fellows like Dewitt in business. She should have done some checking."

"I suppose so," Della said, "but somehow you just can't blame her."

"Well," Mason said, "we're probably a good two hours ahead of them. We'll land at Yuma and take a good long look at Dewitt when he comes driving up to the border."

"What will he do?" Della Street asked.

"He'll answer a lot of questions," Mason said, holding

the oblong of tinted paper in his hands. "A check payable to Millicent Ostrander for one hundred and fifty dollars with no funds. He'll have a chance to do quite a bit of explaining."

"Remember," Drake cautioned, "that Mrs. Ostrander is friendly. She doesn't want to prosecute or make any trouble."

"But she did authorize you to collect on the check?"

"Yes, she did that."

The billowing waves of the sand dunes cast long shadows in the late afternoon sunlight as the plane started losing altitude. The Colorado River, once a twisting serpent of water, now merely a succession of lakes imprisoned behind dams, became a mere trickle under the bridge as the plane crossed into Arizona. They came to a landing at the airport just as the sun was setting.

A man, waiting for them at the gate, gave a sign to Paul Drake.

Drake said, "One of the affiliated agencies over here, Perry. We work together."

The man shook hands and introduced himself.

"Everything okay?" Drake asked.

"Okay," the man said. "We put a man on watch at the border checking station. Only two cars with Massachusetts licenses have been through since then, and neither of them was the one you wanted."

"I'm satisfied we're well ahead of them," Mason said.

Mason turned to the pilot. "You'd better get your plane taken care of and then keep in touch with this detective agency by telephone. We'll let you know when we want to go back. You're licensed to fly at night?"

The man nodded. "Take you back any time."

They got in the car, and the Arizona operative drove them to the Arizona State Line checking station where all cars coming into Arizona were briefly checked for agricultural products which might be contaminated.

Here another operative came forward to meet them, introduced himself and assured them that the car they wanted had not crossed the border.

The group settled down for a long wait.

"No need for you to stay here, Della," Mason said. "You can go up to town and look around. There are some excellent Western and curio shops up here. You can get Indian goods, stamped leather and souvenirs. They'll be open until—"

She interrupted him with a shake of her head. "I'm going to wait right here," she said. "I think, when it comes to the showdown, Aunt Lorraine would rather have a woman in the party. You men are pretty grim and purposeful. You don't any of you impress me as having a good shoulder to cry on."

"How about the man at the checking station?" Mason asked the Arizona detective.

"Oh, he's all right, he's accustomed to it; besides there is nothing he can do. We can wait here if we want to, but he's a good scout. I know him; he'll co-operate."

A steady stream of cars poured across the interstate bridge, down the highway, stopped briefly at the checking station. Paul Drake, with binoculars, sized up each of the oncoming cars, looking quickly at the license numbers.

After an hour, a car with a Massachusetts license came along, and in a flash Drake, Mason and the Arizona detective went into action.

The men stood in the background while the agent at the Arizona checking station asked a few pertinent questions, then returned to the car.

"False alarm," Drake said, stretching and yawning. "How are you folks making out?"

"Fine," Della Street said.

Drake grinned. "This is the part of the job they don't tell you about in the movies, but it's the part that takes up most of the time, leg work and waiting."

Again they settled down in the car.

Big, summer flying beetles started buzzing in a cloud around the glaring lights of the checking station.

"Do you suppose there's a chance they may not cross to-night?" Mason asked Paul Drake.

Drake shrugged his shoulders.

"Aunt Lorraine from Massachusetts," Della Street said, "would be almost certain to observe the proprieties."

Mason settled down in the seat, said, "Sometimes they fool you."

"Surprising how fast you get dehydrated in this climate," Drake said. "You don't know you're perspiring because the perspiration evaporates just as soon as it comes to the surface of the skin but you can lose a gallon of water pretty fast. I could go for one of those root beer floats across the street."

"Go ahead," Mason said. "I'll keep watch and—"

"Hold everything," Drake said suddenly. "We've got a customer."

"Isn't that a California license?" Mason asked.

"It's a California license," Drake told him, the binoculars at his eyes, "and it's a rented car being driven by none other than the boy friend, George Keswick Latty."

"Well, what do you know?" Mason said.

Drake said, "Let me talk with him, Perry, and then if the situation seems to call for it, I'll give you the high sign and you come on over."

"What do you suppose *he's* doing *here*?" Della Street asked.

"I don't know," Drake said, putting the binoculars down on the car seat, "but we're certainly going to find out."

The detective strode across to the car with the California license as the border men flagged it to a stop.

Mason, watching Latty's face, saw the look of amazement which came over the young man's features. Then, after a few moments' conversation, Drake signaled.

The lawyer flung the door of the car open.

"Don't slam it," Della Street warned. "I'm coming."

Mason turned back in time to catch the closing door and get a flash of her legs as she slid across the seat and jumped to the ground.

Her hand clamped on his arm. "I wouldn't miss this for anything," she said.

Latty, talking earnestly with Paul Drake, shifted his eyes over toward the couple approaching him, then his jaw sagged.

"For heaven's sake," he exclaimed, as Mason and Della Street walked up to the car.

"What's the matter?" Mason asked.

"I . . . I didn't have any idea— You people amaze me."

"What's amazing about it?" Mason asked.

"The idea of you being here. I . . . I thought . . . well, I thought you were at least two hundred and fifty miles away."

"No, we're here," Mason said. "And probably you'd better drive over and park your car by ours so we can talk without blocking the station."

They walked alongside Latty's car while he moved it slowly over to the place where the car of the Arizona detective was parked.

Della Street, walking along beside the car, said in a low voice to Mason, "Look at his face. He's thinking desperately."

"I know," Mason said. "We had to give him this much time."

Latty brought the car to a stop.

"Come on," Mason said, opening the door on the driver's side. "Get out and let's see what this is all about."

"I don't understand just what you're doing here," Latty said to Mason.

"And I don't understand just what *you're* doing here," Mason said.

Latty laughed. "Well, it's sort of a mutual surprise, a—"

Mason said, "Latty, quit stalling. Let's have it right on the line and let's have it now."

"Who's stalling?" Latty asked.

"You're trying to," Mason said, "and the more you stall, the more suspicious your actions become. Where's Linda?"

"Back in Los Angeles."

"Where did you get this car?"

"I rented it."

"Did she give you the money?"

"No."

"Where did you get the money?"

"That's none of your business."

"I think it is. Where did you get the money?"

"All right, if you want to know, I had a little nest egg saved up."

"Saved from what?" Mason asked.

"All right," he flared, "from my allowance, if you want to put it that way."

"Did Linda know about that nest egg?"

"No."

"All right, you rented a car. At ten cents a mile that's going to run into money. You must have had a nice little nest egg saved up. Now, what are you doing here? Are you and Dewitt working together?"

The surprise on Latty's face was obvious. "Working together?" he echoed. "Working with that con artist? Certainly not. I'm trying to prevent a murder, that's what *I'm* doing."

"And why did you come here?"

"Because I followed Aunt Lorraine's car to within fifteen miles of here. That's what I'm doing here, and as far as the money is concerned, I hadn't any idea it was going to be this big a trip. I thought I could rent a car and shadow them just to sort of find out what was going on—and then they started driving out of town and I fell in behind them and— Well, it turned out to be quite a trip. I don't know whether they're starting back for Massachusetts or—"

"They're coming across the state line to get married," Mason said. "Arizona will honor premarital health certificates on California forms. They can get married immediately."

"Oh," Latty said, "I see."

"You didn't know that?" Mason asked.

Latty shook his head.

"All right, you followed them to within fifteen miles of here. Then what happened?"

"I lost them."

"What do you mean, you lost them?"

"As soon as it got dark, I was in a bad spot. I could tag along while it was daylight and they didn't know I was following them. Sometimes I'd drop way behind. Sometimes I'd get up closer.

"They stopped for gas back there at Brawley, and I went on a block down the street, pulled in and tried to get my tank filled, but the attendant was busy with another car and the driver of that car wanted every little thing done. By the time the attendant got to my car, they had gone on past so I just paid him for the gas that was actually in my car, about two and a half gallons, then took off after them.

"I didn't know what to do. My gas tank was almost empty. I'm just about out of money and— Well, it looked to me as if they were starting back for Massachusetts. I was going to stop here in Yuma and telephone Linda for instructions and ask her to come and pick up the car and wire me enough money for plane fare home."

"But you lost them?" Mason asked.

"They knew I was following them after I had to turn the headlights on. This man, Dewitt, didn't use the rearview mirror much. He just kept on going, and I don't think he had any idea he was being followed until after it got dark and then I made the mistake of trying to keep too close behind him so he wouldn't get away.

"First he slowed down for me to pass and there was nothing else for me to do; I had to pass. Then I pulled into a gas station as though I were going to get gas, and he went on by me and then I got on his tail again, but he spotted me right away that time and pulled off to the side and slowed down for me to pass.

"So I went on ahead trying to pretend that I wasn't the least bit interested in him and went on about five miles down the road and came to another service station. I pulled

32

in there and waited for him to pass and— Well, he didn't pass, that's all."

"So then what?"

"So then I went back along the road looking for them, but I saw that wasn't any good because the headlights of approaching cars would blind me and— Well, frankly, I don't know whether they passed me or not. I don't think they did, but after half a dozen cars had passed me, I saw that wasn't any good so I turned around and decided to come on to Yuma and telephone."

Mason said, "You've *really* messed things up! We knew they were coming here to get married and we were waiting to intercept them and give this man Dewitt a shakedown. Now we've lost our lead, thanks to your bungling. Shadowing is a job for a professional. When an amateur tries to play detective, he simply messes things all up."

"I'm sorry," Latty said.

The lawyer turned to Paul Drake. "What's your best guess, Paul?"

Drake shrugged his shoulders. "They could have done any one of a dozen things. The probabilities are they simply doubled back to Holtville, Brawley or perhaps Calexico. They'll spend the night there, come on over here tomorrow and get married—or they may go back and have dinner and then come over here to Arizona. You can't tell."

"I must telephone Linda," George Latty said. "She'll be frantic."

"What do you want to tell her?"

"I want to tell her what happened."

"And you want to get back?" Mason asked.

"I've *got* to get back and— Well, I haven't enough money. I want her to wire me funds and that's going to take awhile. I . . . I'm sorry, I guess I just botched things all up."

"You got a good look at Dewitt?" Mason asked.

"I saw him, yes, several times."

"You watched his apartment?"

"No, I was simply shadowing Lorraine Elmore's car."

Mason glanced significantly at Paul Drake.

"All right, Latty," he said, "you've done enough interfering."

The lawyer reached in his pocket, pulled out a billfold, said, "Here's twenty dollars. Go in to Yuma. Drive through the city and on to the Bisnaga Motel. Register there under your own name. Since you're here, we *may* be able to use you. Have a snack and wait for my call. We have reservations and will be there later on, but we may call you at any time. You're willing to help?"

"I'll say I am. I'll do anything you want."

"All right," Mason told him, "you've loused it up this far. Now try to follow instructions and *don't* mess things up any more."

Latty said, "I don't want to make suggestions but shouldn't you start looking for them—tonight?"

"I'm trying to protect her life, not her virtue," Mason said shortly. "If they know they're being followed, that may make them a little cautious."

"Or it may make *him* desperate," Latty said.

"You should have thought of that before you left Los Angeles," Mason snapped. "Now get on to that motel and wait for our call."

Latty flushed. "You're treating me like a child, Mason. I want you to understand that it was my judgment, my influence, my advice and my initiative which got Linda to come to you in the first place."

"All right," Mason said, "I'm not going to argue with you about that because I don't know anything about it and it doesn't make any difference. All I want you to do is to take that initiative of yours, that perspicacity, that decision, and park them at the Bisnaga Motel until we can get this thing worked out. You've heard the old story about too many cooks spoiling the broth. If the broth isn't already spoiled, we'll take over."

Mason moved away from the car, followed by Della Street.

Paul Drake jerked his thumb down the road. "That-a-way," he said.

Latty flushed angrily, said, "All right. Just remember that you've now taken the *sole* responsibility."

He stepped on the throttle, and the car leaped ahead with the tires squealing a high-pitched protest.

"So what do we do now?" Drake asked.

Mason said, "We go and get some dinner. We leave the Arizona operatives here. The minute they pick up that car, they notify us."

"Suppose they double back, leave the car in Holtville, Brawley or El Centro and rent a car and come on here and get married in that?"

"Then we're licked," Mason said. "Even if we stayed here that would lick us, because we don't know Dewitt and we don't know Lorraine Elmore. The Massachusetts car license was our only sure lead. We can, of course, tell the operatives to check on any car that's driven by a man with a patch over one eye.

"However, now that they've been alerted, they can get around us in a variety of ways. For instance, they could simply park their car at El Centro and get on the first bus going to Yuma.

"Instruct the Arizona detectives to cover as best they can. If they spot the car with the Massachusetts license number and the two people in it, or if they pick up the trail of a man with a patch over one eye, let them get in touch with us. When they do, I want to handle it myself. I want to be exceedingly careful that we don't give this man a foundation for a damage suit."

Drake said, "Okay, I'll instruct the men. That idea of a dinner sounds good to me."

Drake talked with the Arizona detectives, then said, "We'll have to get a cab to go to town, Perry, and leave the detectives on duty here."

Mason nodded.

Drake phoned for a cab and gave the driver the name of the restaurant the detectives had recommended.

When they entered the place Drake said to the cashier, "My name is Paul Drake; this gentleman is Perry Mason.

35

We are expecting a telephone call. Will you remember the names and if the call comes in, let us know?"

"I'll be glad to," the cashier said. "What is it, Drake and Mason?"

"That's right, Paul Drake, Perry Mason."

"All right, I'll see that you're called to the phone if anything comes in. Take that table over there in the corner, if you please. There's a phone jack on the wall there and we can have the call transferred right to your table."

As they seated themselves at the table, Paul Drake said, "I'm so hungry I can taste it, but if I order a steak it will take fifteen or twenty minutes to get it and I suppose that call will come just as we're getting ready to eat."

"Let it come," Mason said. "We'll simply have the Arizona detectives follow the parties. If they go to a motel, that's one thing. If they go to a justice of the peace to try to get a marriage fixed up, that will be something else."

Mason said to the waitress who came to the table, "You'd better bring three lobster cocktails that we can nibble on while we are waiting; plenty of green olives and celery. We want three of your best steaks, all medium rare, lots of coffee and we're in a hurry. We'll have our salad with the meal."

The waitress nodded and withdrew.

"Well," Drake said after the waitress had left, "this is going to be a surprise to my stomach *if* I get it. My hunch is that phone will ring just as the steaks are being brought in. It will be a rush emergency and we'll scramble out of here with the steaks left on the table."

"She's bringing the lobster cocktails now," Mason said, "so we'll at least have that much to go on."

They ate their lobster cocktails in silence, nibbled on olives and celery and then Drake, looking toward the kitchen door, said, "Here she comes with the steaks. Come on, telephone!"

The waitress put the covered dishes down on a serving table, picked up the first one with a napkin, placed it in front of Della Street and, with a flourish, removed the silver cover. The appetizing aroma of steak and baked potato filled the air.

The cashier, coming up behind Paul Drake, said, "It's a call for you, Mr. Drake. Here's the phone."

Drake groaned, picked up the telephone, said, "Yes, yes, hello. Paul Drake talking . . ."

"Just a moment," the cashier said. "I have to plug it in; there you are."

"Hello!" Drake said. "Hello, this is Drake . . . yeah . . ."

Della Street said, "Pardon me, folks," and grabbing her knife and fork, cut into her steak. "I'm going to see that this isn't a *total* loss."

The waitress put the platter down in front of Mason, removed the cover. "How about him?" she asked. "Want to wait until he's finished telephoning?"

"No," Mason said, "emphatically not. Serve him now."

Drake pushed the phone a little to one side, nodded to the waitress, said into the telephone, "You're not sure . . . ? Nothing else new . . . no sign of our people? . . . We'll be out of here within twenty minutes or so."

He cradled the receiver, pushed the phone to one side, grabbed knife and fork and attacked the steak.

"Well?" Mason asked.

Drake didn't answer him until he had a mouthful of the savory meat, then he mumbled, "Nothing important. It can wait."

"How long?" Mason asked.

"Until I've finished this steak," Drake said, "and if anybody watches my table manners and sees me wolfing the food, they can stare and be damned."

"We're not standing on ceremony, Paul," Della said.

Drake kept feeding steak and potato into his mouth.

"What sort of dressing on your salad?" the waitress asked.

"Thousand Island," Della Street said.

Mason held up two fingers. "Make it two."

"Three," Paul Drake mumbled.

At length Drake looked at his watch, swallowed, took a

gulp of water, said, "Well, this certainly is a surprise. I never expected to get this far. That call, Perry, was from one of the Arizona operatives at the checking station and he says he saw a car going out, headed back to California, that he thinks it was the same car we checked coming in—that is, the one George Latty was driving. He wanted to know if he should send someone after Latty or just concentrate on the job there. I told him to stay there until we called."

Mason's eyes narrowed. "He wasn't certain?"

"No, it was just a glimpse and something of a hunch."

"No sign of the Massachusetts car?"

"No sign of the Massachusetts car.

"They've made a hurried check of two buses which came through without spotting anyone with a patch over his eye, but they can't really cover those buses and keep a check on the people coming through in cars and, of course, they're concentrating mostly on the cars."

Mason pushed back his chair, leaving the last half of his steak unfinished, walked to the cashier's desk, said, "Could you get the Bisnaga Motel on the line and put the call on the phone there at our table?"

"Certainly, Mr. Mason. I'll be glad to."

Mason went back to his steak and a moment later when he had a signal from the cashier, picked up the phone. "Bisnaga Motel?" he asked.

"That's right," a man's voice said.

"I wonder if you have a George Latty there?" Mason said. "He would have registered within the last hour."

"How do you spell it?"

"L-a-t-t-y."

"Just a minute. Let's see. . . . No, no Latty."

"You're not holding any reservation for a Latty?"

"Just a minute, I'll check that. . . . Nope, no Latty. Not staying here and not any reservation."

"Thank you," Mason said. "I'm sorry I bothered you. I'm rather anxious to get in touch with him."

"That's what we're here for," the man said. "Glad to be of any assistance. Sorry I couldn't locate him for you."

38

Mason pushed back the telephone. His face was grim.

"No dice?" Drake asked.

"No dice."

"What does that mean, Perry?"

"Your guess is as good as mine," Mason said. "I'm sorry I gave the guy that twenty bucks."

"He probably called Linda," Drake said, "and she wanted her hand held. I think that has to be the solution."

Mason said, "Probably. He certainly is a card, talking about his allowance and the money he 'saved.' If he doesn't start learning to stand on his two feet, he'll make a hell of a lawyer."

"Assuming he can pass the bar examination," Della Street said.

Mason finished his steak.

A few minutes later they left the restaurant and took a taxi back to the checking station.

"No luck?" Drake asked the Arizona operatives.

"No luck. How long do you want us to stay with it?"

Drake looked questioningly at Perry Mason.

"How long are you good for?" Perry Mason asked.

"All night if you want."

"All right," Mason told him, "we're going to the Bisnaga Motel. They have phones in the rooms. Call either Paul Drake or me the minute you hit pay dirt—and you'd better get another automobile out here so that one of you can follow the subjects and the other one can dash down to the motel to get us. Give us a ring first. We'll sleep with most of our clothes on and be ready to go at a moment's notice."

"You want us to stay on all night?"

"All night," Mason said, "unless we call it off sooner. They can get married at night here?"

"If they've got money and want to spend it, they can get spliced any time, day or night."

"They'll have money," Mason said, "and they'll want to spend it."

"I don't get it," one of the operatives said. "These people aren't minors."

"They're very mature," Mason said, "but I believe there are some statutes in this state providing that an applicant for a marriage license can be put under oath."

"I believe so," the detective said.

"I want to have the prospective bridegroom put under oath and asked about prior marriages," Mason said, "and I'll probably suggest a few additional questions to the clerk who is issuing the license—with a twenty-dollar tip on the side to see he remembers what I'm asking."

"All right," the operative said, "we'll back your play. We just wanted to know how far you wanted to go."

"All the way," Mason said.

They returned to Yuma in the waiting taxi, rented a car and drove to the Bisnaga Motel. Mason called Linda Calhoun on long distance.

"Mr. Mason!" she exclaimed. "Where are you now?"

"Right now we're at Yuma, Arizona," Mason said. "We are checking on incoming cars to see if your aunt is going to marry Dewitt here."

Mr. Mason, *how* did you get there?"

"By airplane."

"That must have been terribly expensive. I wasn't prepared to—"

"Your end of this," Mason interrupted, "is going to run to one hundred dollars and no more. That's going to pay for two days' detective work. The rest of it is on me."

"But why on you?"

"Just a contribution to the better administration of justice," Mason said. "Don't worry about it, Linda. You haven't heard anything more from your aunt?"

"No, but I have met Belle Freeman, the girl Dewitt promised to marry. She's here at the apartment with me now."

"Can she hear what you're saying?" Mason asked.

"Oh, yes."

"Well, don't talk any more than you have to. I can ask questions; you can answer yes or no if it—"

"Oh, she's all right," Linda interrupted. "She was in love

40

with him two years ago but she's over it now. She knows him for what he is. He got her to turn over her savings to him. He said he had a sure-fire investment that would show a profit. He just took her money and skipped out. She wants to get her money back."

"How much?"

"Three thousand dollars."

"That's fine!" Mason said. "We can get her to confront Dewitt with her claim, and that may make your Aunt Lorraine wake up. Is there any chance there is merely a similarity of names?"

"No. This is the man all right. He had lost an eye in some sort of a gun-running expedition and he always wore a black eye patch and posed as a daring soldier of fortune. It attracted women like flies to a honey jar."

Mason said, "You've told her why you're interested?"

"Yes. She's very sympathetic. She'll do just what we say. She wants to help. She's in love with another man now."

"Did you know that George Latty had tried to follow your aunt's car?" Mason asked.

"George? Heavens, no. I've wondered where he was. I've been ringing and ringing and ringing and—"

"You mean that you haven't heard from him?"

"No."

"Well," Mason said, "he was trying to do a little detective work. He'll probably call you. You keep in touch with the phone; we'll call you later. Now, if you want us, we're at the Bisnaga Motel in Yuma."

"Who is us?"

"Paul Drake, my secretary, Della Street, and I."

"Good heavens, Mr. Mason, all of that expense—"

"I told you not to worry about the expense," Mason told her. "Call me if you hear anything."

The lawyer hung up, reported the conversation, then said, "Things are looking up. I'm going to take my shoes off and that's about all. I think we're coming to a showdown."

"I'll be ready on two minutes' notice," Drake said.

Della Street said, "You give me five minutes, Perry, and I'll be on deck."

Mason said, "Look, Della, there's no need for *you* to—"

"I wouldn't miss it for worlds, Perry. All I really need is five minutes, but I must have those five minutes."

"You'll have it," Mason promised.

"Can you give them that much of a time margin— Montrose Dewitt, I mean?"

"I think so," Mason said. "They'll want to get freshened up before the ceremony."

They retired to their rooms. Mason took off his shoes, propped himself up on the bed with the pillows behind his head, smoked a cigarette, started to doze; then, after an hour, was awakened by the strident ringing of the telephone.

"Yes," Mason said, grabbing the instrument.

"Mr. Mason?"

"Yes."

"There's a long distance call for you from Los Angeles. Want it?"

"Put the party on," Mason said.

A moment later he heard Linda Calhoun's voice. "Oh, Mr. Mason, I'm so glad I got you, I . . . I've heard from Aunt Lorraine."

"Where is she?" Mason asked.

"She's at Calexico. Do you know where that is?"

"Yes," Mason said, "that's the town on the border. It's Calexico on one side and Mexicali on the other. Now, you're in your apartment?"

"Yes."

"Alone?"

"No, Belle Freeman is here. She got all excited after I talked with you earlier. We've been sitting up, drinking coffee and getting acquainted. She's fine company."

"I see," Mason said. "I was trying to get the picture. She's friendly?"

"Oh, *very!*"

"All right, now, why did your aunt call you? To tell you she was married?"

"Oh, no. She just wanted to tell me that everything was forgiven, and that she desperately wanted my friendship."

"That," Mason said grimly, "means that they're married. They went across to Mexico and had some sort of a marriage ceremony."

"Oh, Mr. Mason, I hope not! Aunt Lorraine sounded more like herself than she has in a long time. She told me that she regretted very much the scene that she had with me. She told me that she was a little nervous and upset but that things were different now and . . . she said she would be seeing me tomorrow afternoon."

"In the afternoon?"

"Yes."

"Did she say where?"

"Why, no. I suppose here at the hotel."

"Did she tell you where she's staying?"

"The Palm Court Motel."

"Did she say anything about Dewitt?"

"No, and I didn't ask her but . . . the way she talked, the sound of her voice and everything, I'm satisfied she's— Well, if she *had* been married I'm quite certain she would have told me."

"I'm not certain," Mason said. "The way she called you, her apology and all, sounds to me as if she had been married. Have you heard anything from George?"

"Yes," she said shortly.

"What was it?" Mason asked.

"He asked me to transfer twenty dollars to him by telegraph and waive identification."

"Where was he?"

"El Centro."

"Did he wire or phone?"

"He telephoned collect."

"You sent him the money?" Mason asked.

"I'm going to, but I have to go out to do it and I wanted

to talk with you and let you know what was happening before I went out."

"Okay," Mason said, "he's your boy friend and it's your money."

She laughed. "I'm afraid you don't approve of George, Mr. Mason, and I'm quite sure Aunt Lorraine doesn't."

"I'll repeat," Mason said. "He's *your* boy friend and it's *your* money. Did he call you before or after your conversation with your aunt?"

"Just afterwards."

"And you told him where your aunt was?"

"Of course. He asked me if I knew anything, so naturally I told him about her call. I don't approve of George taking off like that. He's going to have some explaining to do. I was worried about him. I'd been calling his room all afternoon."

Mason said, "I feel your aunt is either married now or that she intends to be married early in the morning and then take a plane back to see you."

"I . . . I hadn't thought of it in that way," she said, "but now that I come to think it over— Is there anything we can do, Mr. Mason?"

"I don't know," Mason said. "I'll think it over."

"It would be such a tragedy for her to throw herself away on him," she said.

"I know how you feel," Mason told her. "You'll hear from me tomorrow."

"Thank you so much. . . . Good night."

"Good night," the lawyer said, and hung up.

Mason walked over to the connecting door leading to Paul Drake's room, tapped gently, then opened the door and listened for a moment to the detective's rhythmic, gentle snoring.

"Wake up, Paul," Mason said. "We have some information and we're going to have to act on it."

Drake sat up in bed, rubbing his eyes, yawning prodigiously.

"Huh?" he asked.

Mason said, "Lorraine Elmore and, presumably, Montrose Dewitt are at the Palm Court Motel in Calexico."

Drake digested that information.

"Now then," Mason said, "there's something a little strange about the whole picture. Aunt Lorraine called Linda Calhoun just a few minutes ago, told her that she wanted to be friends, that she was going to see Linda at the hotel tomorrow afternoon."

"Are they married?" Drake asked.

"I'm afraid they are," Mason said, "although it could be they've decided to wait over in Calexico until morning, then come across here and get married, then return to Los Angeles, but I don't think so.

"Remember that they know they were being followed, thanks to George Latty's clumsiness."

"So what do we do?" Drake asked.

"You stay here," Mason said, "and keep in touch with the Arizona detective agency. I'm going to take the rented car and go to Calexico. I'm going to get them out of bed and call for a showdown with Dewitt."

"Do you have enough on him to do that?" Drake asked.

"I think I have enough on him now, what with Belle Freeman and this bad check, so that we have a basis on which we can start asking questions.

"The thing I'm afraid of is that the telephone conversation may have been a ruse to throw Linda off the trail. They may have told her they were staying at the Palm Court Motel simply as a blind, and they may be on their way right now to Yuma.

"Now, if they should cross the border, you're just going to have to get on their trail and be very, very careful. Don't make any accusations. Simply identify yourself and say that you want to know what he meant by leaving his landlady a check that bounced. He'll probably dig right down into his pocket and make that good with cash.

"Then you can ask him if he is the same Montrose Dewitt who took out a marriage license with Belle Freeman, and if he says he is, then ask him if it is true that he

45

still has some three thousand dollars of her money for investment, and whether the investment was ever made and if so, where.

"Be very careful you don't make any direct accusations, Paul—anything that would lay the foundation for a suit for slander or defamation of character."

Drake, fully awake now, said, "All right, Perry, I'll handle it. I'll put the guy on the defensive—and of course you want me to do it in front of the woman."

"I didn't *say* that," Mason said, grinning.

"I just read your mind," Drake said. "What about Della?"

"She's going to have to go with me," Mason said, "because I think I'm the one that will make the contact and I want to have notes of the conversation."

The lawyer crossed over to the other door of the suite and tapped on Della Street's door. "You've got five minutes, Della," he said.

Her voice, drugged with sleep, said, "Okay, chief, I'll be there."

# Chapter 5

As the lights of Calexico appeared, Mason said to Della Street, "You'll have to wake up now, Della. We're here."

She struggled up to an erect position, shook her head, smiled sleepily, said, "I'm afraid I wasn't much company."

"There was no reason for both of us to stay awake," Mason told her.

"What do we do now?" she asked.

"You get your shorthand book and pen all ready to take notes; we go to the Palm Court Motel and get Aunt Lorraine and Montrose Dewitt out of bed."

"The same bed?" Della Street asked.

"That," Mason said, "remains to be seen."

"And then what do we do?"

"Then we ask questions," Mason told her.

"And suppose he doesn't answer them?"

"We keep on asking."

"Would he have the right to throw you out bodily?"

"He'd have that right," Mason said.

"Would you let him do it?"

"No."

"In other words, this may warm up to quite a little scrap."

"It might," Mason admitted, "but remember this: Aunt Lorraine is in love with the guy. Everything we do is for the purpose of showing him up in his true colors. If he wants to get nasty, we handle things in such a way that it's very evident he's the one who is in the wrong. My job is to make our every action seem reasonable, our every request courteous, and if he wants to be mean about it, we put him in such a position that everything he does seems to be unreasonable and discourteous."

"Do you know where the Palm Court Motel is?" Della Street asked.

"We'll find it," Mason said. "It's not such a big city that we can't just drive around and locate it."

"And over there is Mexico?" Della Street asked.

"That's right, right across that border—just through the gate. Everything on the other side of the high wire fence is Mexico."

"They could get married over there?"

"Presumably."

"You think they've done so?"

"I don't know," Mason said. "The case is a little peculiar, but the main thing is to try and get the scales to drop from Aunt Lorraine's eyes."

"And that's going to hurt," Della Street warned.

"It's better for her to be hurt than killed."

"You think she's in that much danger?"

"We wouldn't be here if I didn't."

The lawyer turned at the intersection, said, "I think the motels are up on this street, as I remember it—they'll probably all be dark now. They— Wait a minute, what's that sign down there, Della?"

"That's it!" Della Street said. "It's an illuminated sign: 'The Palm Court.' "

"That's fine," Mason said. "They'll have vacancies, otherwise they wouldn't have left their sign on. And if they have vacancies, the manager won't be too mad when we get him or her out of bed; in fact, we may as well get some units here ourselves and make it all one big family party."

The lawyer drove the rented car to a stop in front of the building marked OFFICE, got out of the car and pressed the bell button.

It was more than a minute before a matronly woman in her late forties, belting a robe around her, opened the door.

She sized Mason and Della Street up.

"A cabin?" she asked.

"Two cabins," Mason said.

"Two?"

"Two."

"Now, look," she said, "one cabin we rent without any questions. We don't ask to see your marriage license, but when you get two cabins—well, we want to be sure everything's all right."

"Everything's all right," Mason said, "otherwise we wouldn't want two cabins. This young woman is my secretary. I'm an attorney here on business."

"Oh, I see. That's all right. Will you just register here, please?"

"By the way," Mason said, "I'm expecting some people here. What unit do the Dewitts have?"

"The Dewitts?"

"Yes."

"Mr. and Mrs.— Oh, you mean Montrose Dewitt! Well, that's strange, they have two units, too. There's a Montrose Dewitt in Fourteen, and a Mrs. Elmore in Sixteen. They came together."

"I see," Mason said, filling out the cards. "Did they say how long they intended to be here?"

"Just overnight."

"That's fine," Mason said. "How much is it?"

"That'll be twelve dollars for the two."

Mason gave her the twelve dollars. She handed him the keys.

"Just park your car in front of the cabins; everything will be all right. Thank heavens those are my last two vacancies. I can shut off the signs and go to sleep."

The lawyer parked the car, carried Della Street's overnight bag into the unit allotted her, said, "Meet me in front of my unit in five minutes, Della."

The lawyer took his own bag from the car, turned on the lights in his cabin, inspected the accommodations, then waited until Della Street came out of her door.

"All ready?"

"Ready."

"Here we go," Mason said. "We'll try Aunt Lorraine first because we want her to hear everything that's said. She's in sixteen."

The lawyer tapped gently on the door of Unit 16.

When there was no answer after the second knock, Della Street whispered, "They're probably both in Fourteen—that's going to prove embarrassing."

"Not to us," Mason said.

He crossed over to Unit 14 and tapped on the door.

"I don't like to do this," Della Street said. "It's trapping her in a most embarrassing position."

Mason said, "She put herself in that position, we didn't. After all, as I told George Latty, we're not trying to protect her morals, we're trying to save her life."

Again the lawyer tapped on the door.

When there was no answer, he looked at Della Street and frowned. "You'll notice, Della, there's no car in the parking spaces in front of these cabins and no car anywhere on the lot that has a Massachusetts license plate."

"Oh-oh," Della Street said. "Does *that* mean they're out getting married?"

"Presumably," Mason said. "I was afraid of this. They knew they were being followed so they doubled back here, Aunt Lorraine placed a telephone call that was intended to lull Linda into a sense of security and get her to call off her shadows. Then they made a break for Yuma. They're probably there by this time, and Paul Drake is probably in it up to his necktie."

"So what do we do?"

"We call Paul Drake. After all, there's not much we can do now by doubling back, because the action will be all over before we could get there."

"Where do we place the call?"

Mason nodded toward a phone booth at the corner. "See if you can get Paul Drake at the Bisnaga Motel," he said. "Use our credit card, Della."

Della Street went into the phone booth, placed the call,

then after a few moments said, "Hello, Paul. Perry wants to talk to you."

Mason stepped into the phone booth, said, "Hello, Paul. I hardly expected to find you there."

"Why not?" Drake asked, his voice thick with sleep. "You told me to stay here."

"But our quarry has left Calexico," Mason said. "I thought they'd have reached Yuma by this time."

"I haven't heard a word."

"They *might* have slipped through," Mason said.

"Not past those operatives," Drake said. "Not in a car with a Massachusetts license."

"Well," Mason said, "that means they've crossed the border down into Mexico. They're probably married by this time. I'm not familiar with the Mexican marriage laws, but it's a cinch they are by this time. Sorry I bothered you, Paul, but I had to check.

"We're at the Palm Court Motel. That's where Dewitt and Aunt Lorraine are registered, but I doubt if they'll ever come back here. I'm in Unit Nine and Della is in Unit Seven. There are telephones in the rooms. If anything happens, call us."

"Okay," Drake said. "And if I don't hear anything more, then what do I do?"

"You can have the pilot bring the plane down to Calexico first thing in the morning," Mason said. "We're probably all washed up as far as this phase of the case is concerned. When we see Aunt Lorraine, she'll be Mrs. Montrose Dewitt."

Mason hung up, said to Della Street, "There's no use waiting up, Della. I'll sit up for a while on the off chance they're coming back. If they're not here by that time, they won't—"

"You'll do no such thing," she interrupted. "I've had a couple of hours' sleep—you haven't had any. You go to bed and . . ."

He shook his head. "I want to think about the situation a bit, Della. I wouldn't go to bed until I'd got it clarified in my mind, no matter what happens. You roll in and I'll see you in the morning. I'll give you a ring."

"I'd like to take over for you, Chief. I can—"

"No, you go to sleep, Della. I want to think this thing over for a while. See you in the morning. 'Night now."

Mason turned out the lights, drew up a chair by the door of his unit and sat there smoking, watching the yard, giving the problem the benefit of frowning concentration.

When the Massachusetts car hadn't shown up by three-thirty, Mason closed the door, undressed, rolled into bed and was almost instantly asleep.

It was six-thirty in the morning when Della Street tapped on Mason's door. "You up?" she asked softly.

Mason opened the door. "Just finished shaving," he said. "How long have you been up?"

"Just got up. Our lovebirds have flown the nest."

"Apparently so," Mason said. "I looked out the window as soon as I woke up. They— Well, *what* do you know!"

"What?" Della Street asked.

Mason nodded in the direction of the rear cabins. "Take a look," he said. "The man just opening the car door. Turn slowly."

"Why, it's George Latty!" Della Street exclaimed, looking over her shoulder.

"It certainly is," Mason said. "Let's see what *he* has to say for himself."

Latty was just opening the glove compartment of his car when Mason said, "Good morning, Latty."

Latty whirled, an expression of startled incredulity on his face. "You!" he exclaimed. "What are *you* doing here?"

"All right, I'll begin all over again the way we did in Arizona," Mason said. "What are *you* doing here?"

"I . . . I had to sleep somewhere."

"You knew Aunt Lorraine was here?" Mason asked.

"Hush," he said. "Not so loud. . . . Come in. They've got the adjoining cabin."

"And they're there?" Mason asked.

"Why, of course."

52

Mason beckoned to Della Street.

They entered Latty's cabin.

"How long have you been here?" Mason asked.

"I don't know. I didn't look at the time."

"The records will show the time."

"All right, I got here a little before midnight, I guess."

"And you've been in your cabin all this time?"

"I went out to . . . well, to look around a bit and I wanted to see Mexico. I—"

"How long have you been out?"

"Quite a while. I just got—I don't know."

"You're a poor liar," Mason said. "Now tell me what you've been doing."

"That is none of your business."

"Now look," Mason said, "apparently you've been trying to play detective again. You've loused this thing up once and now you've loused it up again. Suppose you give me a couple of straightforward answers for a change. When you arrived here, was the car with a Massachusetts license on it parked in front of those cabins?"

"Why, yes. . . . Now, wait a minute— Well, specifically, I don't remember seeing the car."

"You knew that Dewitt and Aunt Lorraine were here?"

"Yes."

"That's why you came here?"

"Well . . ."

Mason said, "I haven't time to do any sparring with you, Latty. You telephoned Linda from El Centro. You got some money transferred to you. You found out, from talking with her, that Aunt Lorraine and Dewitt were here. So then what did you do?"

"I came down here and got the unit that was next to them. They're right in that next unit, and for your information the walls are pretty thin. They can hear everything we're saying."

"If they're there," Mason said.

"They're there."

"Not now, they aren't."

"They were."

"When?"

"When I got in. . . . Well, sometime after I got in I heard them talking."

Mason said, "I have neither the time nor the inclination to try to squeeze the truth out of you drop by drop. Quit stalling and answer my questions. Why didn't you stay in Yuma as I told you to?"

"Because I . . . I didn't want to. And I'm not going to answer any of your questions. I don't like the tone of your voice. Once and for all, Mr. Mason, *I'm* hiring *you. You're* not telling *me* what to do."

"All right, we'll get it straight," Mason told him. "You're not hiring me. You're not hiring anybody. As far as I'm concerned, you're excess baggage. You're a barnacle, a sponge, a parasite. You're a green adolescent trying to act like a man, and you don't know how.

"For your information, I'm washing my hands of this whole business as long as you have anything to do with it. I'm finished. I'm going to call Linda and tell her exactly how I feel."

Mason nodded to Della, turned and walked out.

From the phone booth the lawyer called Paul Drake. "Anything new at your end, Paul?"

"Nothing."

"All right, get the plane," Mason said. "Come to the airport here. Pick me up, then I'll turn in the rented car and we'll go back to Los Angeles. We're washing our hands of the case."

"What's happened?" Drake asked.

"Too damned much boy friend," Mason said, "plus the fact that the fat's all in the fire now. I don't know what's happened and I haven't time to try to get the truth out of him. You come on over and we'll go back to Los Angeles."

Mason got Linda Calhoun on the phone, said, "I'm just reporting progress, Linda. The birds have flown the coop."

"What happened?"

54

"Your boy friend, George, tried to do some more detective work and apparently loused things up."

"What did he do? He's in El Centro; that is, he *was* in El Centro. He's on his way home now."

"No, he isn't," Mason said. "He's right here at the Palm Court Motel. He came down late at night, managed to get the unit that was next to that occupied by Montrose Dewitt and evidently did a little eavesdropping because he told me that the walls were so thin it was possible to hear ordinary conversation in the adjoining units if one listened carefully."

"Well, of *all* things!" Linda exclaimed.

"I don't know what happened," Mason said, "but apparently the units are vacant at this time and—"

"There were two units?" she interrupted.

"That's right—Units Fourteen and Sixteen. And George rented Twelve. Apparently they went out somewhere. George may have tried to follow them and bungled the job, or else they spotted George and decided to move. George is being uncommunicative with me, and I just haven't time to waste finding out just what did happen. I have the feeling he's been up to something and is covering up.

"I have a plane and will be back in Los Angeles within a couple of hours. We've lost all contact with your aunt, and it isn't going to be worth my time or your money trying to re-establish a contact where we have absolutely nothing to go on.

"Your aunt promised that she'd see you this afternoon. Right now that's the best thing we have to work on. I'll be there when she gets in touch with you. Let's hope Dewitt is with her."

"But what about George?" she asked.

"That's your problem," Mason said. "However, I'd like to ask you if you sent him enough money for a round-trip plane ticket?"

"No, just one way."

"Well, you'd better get him started back," Mason said. "I want him out of my hair, and if you'll take a suggestion from me you'll give him bus fare back instead of paying his first-class fare on a jet plane. Let him realize that a man who tries to be a big shot on someone else's money is—"

The lawyer was interrupted by the sound of a piercing scream which penetrated through the closed glass door of the telephone booth.

"What was that?" Linda asked. "It sounded as if someone screamed and—"

The scream was repeated, this time nearer to the phone booth.

Mason opened the door.

A woman carrying a mop in one hand, a pail of water in the other, was running down the parking place toward the road, screaming at the top of her voice.

As Mason stood watching she dropped the pail, and as the pail rolled, clattering across the hard-surfaced parking place, hot soapy water left a steaming trail.

The running woman continued to carry the mop for four more strides, then flung it from her as though it had been contaminated. She ran to the sidewalk, turned right screaming, "Misses Chester! Misses Chester! Murder!"

Then the closing of a door muffled the sound.

Mason took one quick step back to the telephone. "Hold the line, Linda," he said. "Don't let anybody break the connection. Hang on, I'm going to take a look. That woman came out of the door of Fourteen and it's still open."

The lawyer left the glass door of the phone booth open and, with Della Street at his side, sprinted across the parking surface to the partially opened door of Unit 14.

The lawyer looked inside.

The bed was still made, the throw in place, although pillows had been pulled out and propped up against the headboard.

Sprawled on the floor was the fully clothed figure of a man lying partially on his back. A black patch covered one eye. The face had the unmistakable color of death.

"Good heavens," Della Street said, "what's in the other apartment?"

56

Mason looked back over his shoulder, said, "We'll damned soon find out," and took the passkey which the maid had left in the door of Unit 14, turned to the door of Unit 16 and unlocked the door.

Della Street, looking back toward the sidewalk as Mason fitted the key in the lock, said, "You'd better hurry. Here comes the maid and the manager."

Mason unlocked the door, flung it open unceremoniously.

There were several articles of rather expensive luggage which had been opened. The contents were strewn about the room. For the most part these were articles of feminine wearing apparel.

Here again the bed had not been slept in.

"Who are you?" the woman approaching demanded of Perry Mason.

"Perry Mason," the lawyer said, "and this is my secretary. We heard the maid saying there'd been a murder."

"Not in here, not in here," the maid said. "It's the other one—Fourteen."

"Oh, pardon me," Mason said.

"Are you an officer?" the manager asked.

Mason smiled. "I'm a lawyer," he said, stepping back.

The manager looked in the door of Unit 14, then stepped inside the room.

"Well, well," Mason said, as though seeing the corpse for the first time, "apparently there's a dead man— however, I see no indications of murder."

The door of Unit 12 opened, and George Latty, his shirt removed, his face covered with lather, a razor in one hand, stood in the doorway, attired in trousers and undershirt. "What's all the commotion about?" he asked.

Mason ignored the question to say to the manager, "It would seem to be a natural death, but you'd better call the authorities."

The manager backed out of the room, pushing Mason back from the door as she did so. She slammed the door shut, walked over to Unit 16 and pulled that door shut.

A door from one of the other units opened. A man attired

in pajamas and robe said, "What's all the screaming about?"

"Something frightened the maid," the manager said, smiling.

George Latty said to Mason, "What's this all about, Mason?"

Mason turned to look at him. "What's what all about?"

"All the screaming."

"Oh, you heard the screaming?"

"Of course I heard the screaming. It sounded like the whistle of a locomotive."

"And ran right out, just the way you were?"

"Of course."

Mason said, "Was your face lathered before or after you heard the scream?"

"Before, why?"

"Then you must have waited some time before opening the door."

"I . . . I wasn't very presentable."

"You mean you changed clothes?" Mason asked.

"No, I was the way I am now but I . . . I hesitated."

"So I see," Mason said and, turning his back on him, strode rapidly back to the phone booth.

The lawyer picked up the telephone, said, "Are you still on, Linda?"

"Heavens, yes. I've had a fight to hold the line. What is it? What's happened?"

"Apparently," Mason said, "Montrose Dewitt is dead. Your aunt is missing. Someone has apparently gone through all the baggage in both units very hastily and, since George Latty has been in the adjoining unit to that occupied by Dewitt, there will undoubtedly be complications."

"Good heavens, you don't mean there's been a fight? George wouldn't . . ."

"I'm quite satisfied that George wouldn't," Mason said as she hesitated, "but the main problem before the house is what's happened to your aunt— Wait a minute. Does your aunt have reddish hair?"

"Yes."

"I *think*," Mason said, "the woman who has just hurried past me and is approaching the door of Unit Sixteen is— I'll call you later. Good-by."

The lawyer slammed up the phone, sprinted across the parking place.

George Latty had retired behind the door of Unit 12 and closed the door. The manager and the maid were back in the office, presumably telephoning the police.

The woman tried the door of Unit 16, frantically rattled the door, then was starting for 14 when Mason put his hand on her arm.

"Lorraine Elmore?" the lawyer asked.

She whirled to face him with wide, panic-stricken eyes.

"Yes, who are you?"

"I'm an attorney," Mason said, "and I think you'd better talk with me before you talk with anyone else."

"But I have to get in my room and I have to locate my . . . my friend."

"You don't have a key?"

"No."

"Where is it?"

"It was . . . taken."

Mason said, "Please, Mrs. Elmore, come with me. For your information, I am acquainted with your niece, Linda Calhoun."

"With Linda—you?"

"Yes," Mason said, exerting gentle pressure on her arm as he led her across the parking area, "and this is Miss Della Street, my confidential secretary. If you'll just come with us for a few moments, Mrs. Elmore, we may be able to help you, and I think perhaps you're going to need help."

# Chapter 6

As Mason nodded to Della Street, she seated Lorraine Elmore in the overstuffed chair, and Della Street drew up a straight-back chair to take a seat beside her.

Mason stood for a moment, then sat on the edge of the bed. "Can you tell me about it, Mrs. Elmore?"

"You're a friend of Linda's?"

"Yes. She has been in touch with me in connection with another matter. I think she'd be interested in—"

"If you're a friend of Linda's, that's all I need to know. They've murdered Montrose."

"Who has?" Mason asked.

"Enemies," she said vaguely.

"Whose enemies?"

"His," she said and started to cry.

Della Street patted her shoulder. "If you can just let us know what happened, Mrs. Elmore, before giving way to emotion . . ."

"Just give us the bare facts," Mason said.

Lorraine Elmore choked back tears, said, "Oh, we were going to be so happy."

"Never mind," Della Street said. "Please try and tell Mr. Mason exactly what happened."

She said, "It was terrible. We were just trying to live our own lives, to start out by ourselves in search of our own happiness, to begin all over again and—"

"Can you just please tell me what happened," Mason asked, "just the events, Mrs. Elmore."

"We were followed," she said, "and Montrose became deathly afraid. He said there were people who . . . who had it in for him and . . ." Again she started to cry.

Mason said, "All right, Mrs. Elmore, I'm going to have to question you. Please answer my questions briefly and to the point. Where's your car?"

"Out there," she said, with a vague motion of the wrist.

"Where?"

"On a dirt road."

"Where?"

"Miles from here."

"How far?"

"I don't know."

"How long did you drive before you abandoned your car?"

"It happened about . . . about twenty minutes, I guess, after we left here."

"What time did you leave here?"

"I don't know, perhaps around midnight."

"Why?"

"That same car that had been following us was parked in the parking space. Montrose recognized it."

"Did he know who was driving it?"

"No."

"But it had been following you?"

"Yes."

"You're sure?"

"Of course. The man had stopped in a gasoline station to let us go by and then tried to pick us up again and we slowed down and let him drive past us."

"You didn't recognize the driver?"

"Why should I recognize him? I'm from Massachusetts. This is California. Anyway, I was on the right side. He passed on the left."

"I see," Mason said. "So you and Montrose got in your car. Where were you going?"

"He wanted to talk. We wanted to make plans and we thought we were being spied upon, so we went out to park where we could talk without being interrupted and without anyone overhearing us."

"Where?"

"We went out on the pavement and then turned off on a dirt road."

"Do you know which way you went on the pavement?"

"The way we had come in."

"Toward Yuma?"

"Yes, I guess so. It was in that direction."

"And then what happened?"

"Well, we came to a dirt road that led off to the side and we turned off on it and parked."

"How far did you go on it before you parked?"

"I don't know, just a little ways—just far enough to get away from the highway."

"You walked back?" Mason asked.

"That was after . . . afterwards."

"After what?"

"After the man made Montrose get out of the car."

"All right," Mason said. "You were parked. You were sitting there talking and what happened?"

"This car drove up behind us. It didn't have any lights. We didn't notice it until it was right on top of us, and then Montrose opened the door and started to get out and this man was standing there with a handkerchief over his face. You couldn't see a thing—that is, what he looked like—just a thin white handkerchief hanging down from his hatband over his face, and he said, 'Get out,' and pushed the gun out right in front of Montrose."

"You saw the gun?"

"Yes, yes! It was moonlight, and I saw the moonlight glinting from the blue steel on the gun."

"Then can you tell me what happened?" Mason asked. "And please hurry as much as you can—it's important."

"The man told me to stay there, and he and Monty walked back and all of a sudden Monty tried to get the gun from him, and he clubbed Monty, and Monty fell down, and then the man just stood over him and clubbed him, and clubbed him, and clubbed him— Oh, it was terrible, terrible, terrible! I just—!"

"Now hold it," Mason said. "You're getting hysterical.

What happened? Never mind your emotions, we have to know."

"Well, the man left Monty there sprawled out by the side of the road. He was dead. I know he was dead. Such a horrible clubbing! You could hear the sound of the blows and—"

"All right, the man came back to the car. Then what?"

"He got in beside me, searched around the inside of the car and through the glove compartment. Then he grabbed my handbag and told me to drive the car straight ahead."

"Now, that was in the direction that was away from the highway?"

"Yes."

"You were on a dirt road?"

"Yes."

"And the man sat behind you?"

"No, he went back to his car and got in it and drove right behind me."

"With lights on?"

"No, he still had his lights off."

"And the handkerchief over his face?"

"Yes."

"Then what happened?"

"I kept on driving until he blew on the horn and turned on the lights, and then I stopped and he got out of the car and said, "Now, Sister, drive straight on, just as far as you can go."

"Then what?"

"Then he got in his car and started backing up."

"And what did you do?"

"Just what he told me to, only it was what I wanted to do anyway because I wanted to get away from him. I saw him start backing his car and turning around and, believe me, I put my car into gear and stepped on the throttle and just started flying down that road."

"And what happened?"

"All of a sudden there was sand all over the road, and I

started skidding and I guess I lost my head. I raced the wheels and just dug a hole and the motor stalled."

"When what?"

"I tried and tried to get the car out but I couldn't. The wheels just kept digging deeper and deeper in that sand."

"So what did you do?"

"I waited awhile and then I started walking back."

"And you walked back the way you had come in?"

"Yes."

"Now," Mason said, "this is important. Did you recognize the place where the man had stopped you when you came to it?"

"No, I just kept on walking. I just followed the road. I kept thinking I would see Monty lying there . . . his body . . . but the man had loaded the body in the car and taken it away with him."

"You didn't hear any shot being fired?" Mason asked.

"No."

"And what happened to you?"

"I walked and walked until I got tired and then I just had to rest. I had sand and gravel in my shoes and I guess somewhere I got lost. I got off on a side road somewhere and I wandered around in sand hills and . . . finally I came to the highway and after what seemed like hours a man gave me a ride."

"Let's see your feet," Mason said.

She held up her foot.

"I took off my stockings," she explained. "They got all snagged and worn and I just walked in my shoes."

Mason slipped off the shoe, looked at the rawness of the blistered feet, said, "You saw this man beating Montrose Dewitt?"

"Heavens, yes! I saw him and I heard him. Oh, it was terrible. He clubbed and clubbed and after Monty was down and lying still he just clubbed him and kicked him and—"

"But no shot?" Mason asked.

"No, I didn't hear any shot."

Mason said, "I want you to sit right there, Mrs. Elmore, and rest. My secretary and I have to put through a phone call."

"I . . . I'll use the bathroom," she said and got up out of the chair, started to take a step and would have fallen if Mason hadn't held her.

"Oh, my feet!" she said. "My poor feet."

"Take it easy," Mason told her.

She hobbled to the bathroom, closed the door.

Mason said to Della Street, "Della, she's lying."

"How do you mean?"

"I saw the body," Mason said. "There isn't a mark on the face, nothing to indicate the man had been clubbed. I don't know how he died, but if she tells that story . . . we just can't let her tell it."

"How can we stop it?"

Mason said, "Look, Della, this is the time when we need someone who knows the ropes. There's a lawyer here that I've worked with named Duncan Crowder. You go to the outside telephone, get him on the line, and tell him to come here at once. Tell him I want him to work with me on a case. Tell him to drop anything he's doing and get here fast."

Della Street nodded, said, "Suppose he isn't in?"

"If he isn't in we're sunk," Mason said, "because I don't know any other lawyer I can trust. Crowder is a seasoned campaigner."

The lawyer moved over to the window, moved the drapes back, looked out.

There were several cars parked in front of Unit 14, and a dozen or so people were gathered in a little group near the door.

When Della Street came back, Lorraine Elmore was still in the bathroom.

"Get him?" Mason asked.

"I got him and he's on his way down. He wanted to take time to explain something to me, but I told him there

65

wasn't time for anything, to just get down here; that you wanted him and wanted him right away."

"Good girl," Mason said. "Now . . ."

He broke off as the bathroom door opened and Lorraine Elmore, looking wan and drawn, started limping toward the chair.

Della hurried to her side.

"Wouldn't you like to lie down a little while?" she asked.

"Yes," Mrs. Elmore said. "I took some pills last night and then . . . I guess . . . I must have dozed— Oh, I want to forget! Can you get me some medicine to quiet me?"

Della Street escorted her to the bed, stretched her out, said, "Now just lie there and I'll soak a towel with cold water and put it over your eyes."

Mrs. Elmore smiled gratefully and said, "I . . . I have to tell the police. It—"

"There's time for that later," Mason said. "Take care of her, Della."

The lawyer hurried outside and into the phone booth. He rushed through a call to Linda Calhoun.

When she answered, Mason said, "Linda, this is Perry Mason. Now I want you to listen and get this—"

"Mr. Mason, whatever in the world has happened? What's happened to Aunt Lorraine? What's—"

"Shut up," Mason said, "and listen. Listen carefully. Montrose Dewitt is dead. Your aunt has been through a harrowing experience. According to her story he was clubbed to death before her eyes. But your aunt is hysterical and upset. There are certain things that don't fit into the picture. The story she tells is simply— Well, frankly, it isn't convincing."

"Aunt Lorraine wouldn't lie," Linda said.

"Are you sure?"

"Well, I . . . I'm reasonably sure."

"Not even if someone told her to?"

"If . . . if she's in love and—"

Mason said, "There's something about this I don't under-

66

stand. Now, is it all right with you if I represent your aunt? She needs a lawyer and she needs one now."

"Why, of *course* it's all right! That's what I wanted you to do all along, Mr. Mason. I wanted you to—"

"Now, wait a minute," Mason said. "This is where the catch comes in. If I'm representing your aunt, I'm not representing you and I'm not representing George."

"But I want you to represent my aunt and— Well, what does George have to do with it?"

"I don't know," Mason said. "George may or may not know something. If I'm representing your aunt, she's my client. Now, do you want me to represent her or not?"

"Yes, yes, please, Mr. Mason."

"All right," Mason said, "stick by the telephone. I'll report to you as soon as there's anything to report."

"Shouldn't I come down there? Shouldn't I—"

"I think you should," Mason said. "You'll probably have to charter a plane unless you have someone who can drive you down."

A man standing outside the telephone booth tapped on the glass door, called in, "I'm a reporter, Buddy. I've got to rush a story in to my paper. How's for giving me a break?"

"Okay," Mason said, and then into the telephone, "I'll call you later."

He hung up and opened the door of the phone booth. The reporter hurried past him and started dialing a number.

Mason went back to his room, opened the door gently to see Della Street sitting on the edge of the bed, holding a wet towel over Lorraine Elmore's forehead and eyes.

Della Street raised her finger to her lips, motioning for silence.

Mason quietly moved over to the window, looked out on the parking place and the people who were standing in groups.

A knock sounded at the door.

Lorraine Elmore started to raise up on the bed.

"Now, just keep quiet," Della Street said. "It's all right."

Mason went to the door, said, "Who is it?"

A man's voice said, "It's Duncan Crowder, Mr. Mason."

The lawyer opened the door, a welcoming smile on his face, then suddenly stiffened. The young man who stood on the threshold was fully as tall as Mason. He had dark, wavy hair; steady slate-colored eyes; even, regular features, and a reassuring smile.

Mason said, "*You're* not the man I sent for."

The visitor said, "I tried to explain to your secretary that my father is in the hospital. I'm taking over as best I can. She didn't give me a chance to tell her anything, but said to get down here at once and then hung up."

"I see," Mason said thoughtfully. "I'm sorry to hear about your father. You have a partnership?"

"That's right—Crowder and Crowder. I'm Duncan Crowder, Junior."

Mason said to Della Street, "Is your unit open, Della?"

She nodded.

"We'll talk there," Mason said, and stepping outside appraised the young man.

"I'm sorry," Crowder said, as Mason gently closed the door. "I gathered it was a matter of great urgency. There was no opportunity for making explanations over the phone so I thought I'd come and explain personally."

"How long have you been practicing?" Mason asked.

"About two years, Mr. Mason. I've heard my father speak of you many times and I feel that I know you. I've followed your cases in the papers—as who hasn't?"

"All right," Mason said, leading the way to the unit which had been occupied by Della Street and opening the door. "Come on in and sit down. You're going to learn something about the practice of law that isn't contained in the books."

"You want me to work with you?" he asked.

Mason nodded.

"What is it?" Crowder asked.

Mason took out a billfold and said, "Here, I'm giving you a dollar. You're retained. There'll be a further fee forthcoming. I don't know how much it's going to be. I don't know how much my fee is going to be. But now you've been properly retained so there's a professional relationship."

Crowder gravely took the dollar, pocketed it and said, "Go ahead."

Mason said, "There's a dead man in Unit Fourteen. There's a possibility he's been murdered. I don't know.

"What I do know is this: Lorraine Elmore, who is our client, is in there in a state of hysteria. We've managed to get her quiet now. She thinks she witnessed the murder."

"In the motel?" Crowder asked.

"*Not* in the motel," Mason said. "That's the trouble with her story. It is a weird, somewhat improbable story and when you tie it in with the physical facts it's completely contradictory to the evidence. I don't want her to tell that story and yet, if she doesn't tell it, she's going to be in as bad a position as if she did tell it.

"Therefore, there's only one thing to do."

Crowder looked Mason in the eyes, thought for a long moment, then said, "You mean we want a good doctor."

Mason said, "Young man, you have a remarkable legal mind. I guess you're a chip off the old block.

"There are two reasons why I need a local attorney on the job. In the first place I need a doctor, and in the second place I want someone who can get in touch with a coroner, the newspaper reporters and the local people and get the facts of the case before our client has to do any talking."

Crowder said, "How about this phone—is it connected?"

"It goes through a switchboard of some sort in the office," Mason said, "and your call will be monitored. There's a phone booth outside."

Crowder nodded, stepped to the door, then came back and shook his head. "They're lined up three deep in front of that phone booth," he said.

"Okay," Mason told him, "we'll use this phone. Be careful what you say."

Crowder picked up the phone and after a moment said, "May I have an outside line, please? . . . Oh, I see, if you have to dial the numbers, I want—I don't remember his number and I don't have a phone book here, but it's Dr. Kettle. . . . Would you ring him, please?"

There was a period of silence, then Crowder said, "Horace, this is Duncan Crowder, Junior. I'm down here at the Palm Court Motel in Unit Seven. Now, that's near the street as you turn into the parking place on the right-hand side. I want you to get down here right away. Yes, *right* away. . . . Sure it's an emergency—no, not surgical, but I want you here just as fast as you can get here. . . . Okay."

Crowder hung up and said, "He'll be here right away. Incidentally, Dr. Kettle does a lot of autopsy work for the coroner."

"I see," Mason said. "I take it that he's friendly to you?"

"Very friendly. He's a client and Dad's personal physician."

"Yours?" Mason asked, grinning.

Crowder matched his grin. "I haven't needed one yet."

Mason said, "The dead man is Montrose Dewitt. Our client is Lorraine Elmore. She's a widow from Massachusetts. There's every indication that Dewitt was a crook—one of the type who preys on women—and there *may* be a more sinister angle to it."

"Murder of his victims?" Crowder asked.

Mason nodded.

"And what happened to him?"

"He's dead," Mason said. "He was found lying on the floor of Unit Fourteen. Our client was in Sixteen. There's also every indication that both Units Fourteen and Sixteen were subjected to a very hasty search. Whoever did the searching apparently had more time in Unit Fourteen. The suitcase is open and some things have been taken out, but there's no indication of disorder.

"In Unit Sixteen, however, the one that was occupied by Lorraine Elmore, the search was apparently more hurried, and feminine wearing apparel has been pulled out of the suitcases and scattered all over the place. Our client may have been carrying a large sum of money in cash.

"I became interested in the case because of a niece of Mrs. Elmore's—a girl named Linda Calhoun—who wanted me to protect her aunt from possible murder."

"And marriage?" Crowder asked.

Mason said, "The more I see of you, Crowder, the more I think you and I are going to get along.

"Now, Linda Calhoun has a boy friend, George Latty, who is here at the motel and has been here since sometime last night. Incidentally he has Unit Twelve, which is immediately adjacent to that occupied by Montrose Dewitt, and he told me that the walls of the units were so thin it was possible to hear conversation in an adjoining unit.

"The numbers are odd on this side and even on the other side, so if Latty heard conversation through the walls it must have been either conversation from Unit Fourteen, or from Unit Ten on the other side."

"He didn't say?" Crowder asked.

"He didn't say and he isn't going to say," Mason said. "What he did say slipped out inadvertently. I think he's going to clam up."

"Any chance he knows anything about it?" Crowder asked.

"Lots of chance."

"What sort is he?"

"He's studying law," Mason said. "He looks as if he spends quite a bit of time looking at himself in a mirror after he's watched some of the current crop of heroes on T.V.

"Linda works," Mason went on, "and evidently makes a fair salary. From that salary she's putting up money for George Latty's education. Now, here's the part that to my mind is indicative of his character: Latty told me that he had a small amount of money saved from his—and I quote—allowance—unquote and that Linda knew nothing about this amount, which evidently represented a surreptitious saving."

"I see," Crowder said. And then after a moment asked, "Sideburns?"

Mason indicated a spot halfway down his cheek. "To here."

"In what respect does our client's story differ from the physical facts?" Crowder asked.

"In quite a few respects," Mason said. "She insists the man was beaten and then clubbed to death out in the desert. Her car is out there somewhere and heavens knows what evidence will have been left in her car. I have a detective due here almost any minute and a chartered airplane. Her description about where she left the car is a little indefinite because she doesn't know the country, but I thought after the doctor gets on the job we could do a little flying and—"

There was a knock at the door.

Mason crossed over to open the door.

The man who stood on the threshold was in his fifties, a small-boned, energetic, poker-faced individual, whose keen eyes surveyed Perry Mason.

"Crowder here?" he asked.

"You're Dr. Kettle?"

"That's right."

"I'm Perry Mason."

Crowder stepped forward and said, "Hello, Doctor. Come in."

Dr. Kettle said, "So you're Perry Mason, the great attorney."

Mason grinned. "I see I must have had a good press agent."

"You have," Dr. Kettle said. "What is it you people want?"

Crowder said, "Do you mind, Mr. Mason?"

"Not at all," Mason said. "Go ahead."

"We have a client in the adjoining unit," Crowder said, "who needs medical treatment. I'd better describe her symptoms."

Dr. Kettle shook his head. "You'd better let me make my own diagnosis."

Crowder said, "*I'd* better describe the symptoms."

"Can she talk?" Kettle asked.

"Yes."

"Then *I'll* get the symptoms."

Crowder said, "*I'd* better describe the symptoms."

Suddenly Dr. Kettle grinned. "I guess I'm a little dense this morning. Go ahead, describe the symptoms."

"This woman," Crowder said, "may or may not have been a witness to a murder. She has gone through a very harrowing experience. She is somewhere in her forties and has become emotionally upset and hysterical.

"Of course, later on it will be necessary for her to tell her story to the police, but at the moment it would be, at least in my opinion as a layman, medically unwise for her to do so."

"Why?" Dr. Kettle asked in a single whiplash question.

"Because she is emotionally upset and hysterical and her recollection may be at variance with some of the physical facts. It would, therefore, be exceedingly unfair to this witness for her to be interrogated while she was in her present emotional state."

"I'll take a look at her," Dr. Kettle said, "but from your description of the symptoms, Duncan, I feel quite sure she's in a state of acute hysteria and it will be necessary to have absolute quiet. I'm going to give her heavy sedation, transfer her to a hospital, put special nurses on the job, see that there are no visitors, and keep her completely quiet for at least twenty-four hours. At the expiration of that time, when she is completely out from under sedation. I'll determine whether it will be advisable for her to make any further statement."

Mason said, "I think, now, Doctor, it's time for you to see the patient."

"I'm quite certain it is," Dr. Kettle said.

"You'll transfer her in an ambulance?" Mason asked.

Dr. Kettle shook his head. "Ambulances attract attention. I'll get her out to my car and take her to the hospital personally; that is, if she can walk."

"I think she can," Mason said. "It will be rather painful."

"Why?"

"She had a long walk in the desert."

"I see."

Mason opened the door of the unit. Dr. Kettle stepped out, looked to the right and left, then walked over toward the adjoining unit.

Mason opened the door, said, "This is my secretary, Della Street, Dr. Kettle. . . . Now, Mrs. Elmore, I have a doctor here who is going to see if he can help you a little bit, and take a look at those feet of yours. We don't want to have any chances of an infection."

Mason said to Della Street, "I think, Della, that it would be better to leave the doctor alone with his patient."

Dr. Kettle, opening his bag, took out a bundle of gauze, unwrapped a hypodermic syringe and said, "Do you feel nervous, Mrs. Elmore?"

Lorraine Elmore pulled the cool bandage from her flushed forehead, tried to struggle to a sitting position.

"Just take it easy," Dr. Kettle said. "I understand you've had a harrowing experience."

Lorraine Elmore nodded, tried to talk, then started to sob.

Dr. Kettle tilted a bottle. The odor of alcohol filled the room. "Just let me have your left arm, if you will, please, Mrs. Elmore."

Mason said, "Just one question, Mrs. Elmore, before Dr. Kettle gives you a shot to steady your nerves. You had a large sum of money with you?"

She gave a convulsive start. "Heavens, yes! I'd forgotten all about it. Monty had a lot of cash with him, too."

"Where is it?" Mason asked.

"I— We— It's under the seat of the overstuffed chair in his cabin. We decided it would be best to hide the money before we went out in the car."

"You talked it over?" Mason asked.

"Yes. We decided we'd leave the money and— Ouch!"

"That's all," Dr. Kettle said, withdrawing the hypodermic needle.

"Will you take care of the money?" Mrs. Elmore asked.

"We'll do the best we can," Mason promised.

74

Dr. Kettle motioned toward the door.

Mason, Della Street and Duncan Crowder moved silently out of the unit.

"I'm sorry," Duncan Crowder said to Della Street, "you didn't give me a chance to explain about my father being in the hospital and the fact that I'm carrying on the business as best I can."

"It's my fault," Della Street said. "We were faced with a real emergency here, and I simply didn't dare take the time to listen. Mr. Mason said to get Duncan Crowder and get him here at once, and when I asked you if you were Duncan Crowder and you said you were, and then went on to say 'but,' I'm afraid I interrupted rather sharply."

"You did," Crowder said, grinning.

Mason said, "Crowder, we have a job to do."

"The money?" Crowder asked.

Mason nodded.

Crowder looked across at the group of curious people milling around the unit which had been occupied by Montrose Dewitt. "If it's all the same to you, Mr. Mason," he said, "I'd suggest you wait here. Your photograph has been published a good many times. People are going to recognize you and start talking.

"Let me go over there and work around the edges of the crowd. I know the coroner and I know the chief of police. I can probably get a look but I couldn't remove anything."

"Go ahead," Mason said. He took Della Street's arm and they stood in the doorway of the cabin Della Street had occupied, watching Duncan Crowder as he moved around in the group exchanging greetings here and there; then they saw him speak to one of the men and step inside, with the calm assurance of a person entering his own home.

Crowder was in there for a good five minutes, then he emerged with crisp, businesslike efficiency. This time he did not pause to talk with the people gathered outside the cabin but strode directly down to where Mason and Della Street were waiting.

"Find it?" Mason asked.

"Nothing," Crowder said.

"You looked under the cushions of the big chair?"

Crowder nodded.

"Any indication that the cushion had been removed from the big chair?"

Crowder shook his head. "No indication that would be any good either way. You can pull the cushion out of the chair and put it back without disturbing anything. However, there's one point that *may* be significant."

"What's that?"

"Quite a bit of small change in the space between the cushion and the chair," Crowder said, "where it *could* have fallen out of the side trousers' pocket of some man who sat there with one leg crossed over the other—the change would have dribbled out. Or it could have been planted there by someone who wanted it to appear the cushions had been undisturbed."

Crowder went on, "Personally I'd give her the benefit of the doubt, but— Well, *what* do you know!"

Mason followed the direction of Crowder's gaze.

"Look at the guy," Crowder said. "They talk about our broad-brimmed hats being conspicuous in Boston. Look at that little capsule perched on that guy's head. It reminds me of when my mother used to make apple pies. She'd pinch the crust off the end of the plate and then trim off that little—"

Mason interrupted him. "Crowder," he said, "get across there quick! That's Howland Brent from Boston. He's Lorraine Elmore's business manager. He must have been occupying one of these units. Find out when he got in here, and under what name he registered— Good Lord, does *this* complicate the situation!"

"On my way," Crowder said. "Keep back in the doorway out of sight, if you will, please, Mr. Mason."

Crowder moved over to the office of the motel, was back in a few minutes, stating, "That's the name, all right; Howland Brent, from Boston, Massachusetts; apparently driving a rented car because it has a California license plate. Registered in shortly before you did last night. He has Unit Eleven. That's next to you."

Mason's eyes were level-lidded with concentration.

"You're beginning to attract attention," Crowder warned. "You somehow stand out in a crowd, and Miss Street is *far* from unattractive. I have noticed a few wolflike glances from the local citizens at the other end of the court."

"I've noticed them myself," Della Street said laughing, "even when I pretended not to."

"I think we'd better leave," Mason said. "I think Mrs. Elmore is in safe hands."

"She won't make any statement for at least twenty-four hours," Crowder promised. "Not with Dr. Kettle on the job. At least, nothing that will be passed on. Anything she says will be a confidential communication to her physician."

"Or a nurse," Mason said.

"Or a nurse," Crowder amended.

"I think we'd better leave," Mason said, "although I *am* waiting for Paul Drake."

"Who's he?"

"The detective I have working on the case. He should be here at any minute."

Crowder said, "All right, we're safe for twenty-four hours. What are you going to do at the end of that time?"

"I wish I knew," Mason said.

Crowder said, "I think you'd better get in your car, drive out to the street, and you can watch for the detective from there."

"Wait a minute," Della Street said, "here's a cab coming now."

"That's Paul," Mason said, reaching an instant decision. "You get in the rented car, Della, and Mr. Crowder can ride with you. I'll get in the cab with Paul."

Mason hurried out to the sidewalk as the cab slowed and started to turn.

Paul Drake was reaching in his pocket.

Mason said, "Keep the cab, Paul. I'm joining you."

The lawyer jerked the door open, jumped in and said to the cabdriver, "Back to the airport, if you will, please."

The cabdriver backed the cab into a turn, said, "Hey, what's happened here? The court is full of people."

"A fight or something, I guess," Mason said, "or maybe someone ran into one of the parked cars. How quick can you get us to the airport?"

"Right fast," the cabdriver said. "Hey, is that car behind following us?"

"It's following us," Mason said. "Those are people who are with us."

"I see."

Drake raised his eyebrows at Mason.

The lawyer warned him to silence with a glance. "Is the plane all ready to go, Paul?"

"All gassed up and ready," Drake said.

"That's fine," Mason told him. "This is going to be a busy day, Paul."

"So I gather," Drake said.

# Chapter 7

As the cars came to a stop at the airfield, Mason approached the pilot.

"You're all ready to go?" he asked.

"Yes."

"Plenty of gas?"

"That's right."

Mason turned to Crowder, said, "Your office has rather a wide acquaintance here in the Imperial Valley?"

"Down at the south end of it," Crowder said.

"And," Mason said, "doubtless some of your clients have property for sale?"

"I'm quite sure they do."

"Know anyone in particular that has property out east of here that would be interested in selling, or wants to sell?"

"Yes, I think I do," Crowder said.

"Could you point out that property from the air?"

"I could try."

"I'm interested in property down here in the valley," Mason explained. "I think it might be a good investment. I'd like to find out something about the topography of the country and just where the sand hills are located. I understand there are some to the east and a little to the north of here. Before I return to Los Angeles it might be a good idea for us to fly over the country."

"I'll go with you," Crowder said. "Later on I'll get some specific pieces of property lined up, together with prices. Right at the moment I can only give you general information."

"General information is all I need," Mason told him. "I think the best thing to do would be to go east of here and

79

follow all of the roads which turn north. That's the section generally that I'm interested in, and I'd like to get an idea of the topography of the country.

"If you'll accompany me and answer any questions I may have, we'll bring you back to the airport."

"I'll be glad to go," Crowder said.

"We're going to have to do some low flying," Mason told the pilot, "and then we may have to take off for Los Angeles without stopping to refuel."

"It's all right," the pilot said. "I can take you anywhere you want to go, within reason."

They climbed into the plane and fastened seat belts. The pilot warmed the motors up, taxied down the field and took off.

"Where to?" he asked.

Mason turned to Duncan Crowder.

"Go east about twelve miles," Crowder said. "Fly over Calexico for a fix, then follow the paved road out toward Yuma."

The pilot nodded. The plane banked into a turn.

As they flew over the motel at Calexico, Mason studied the situation, noticed that a machine of the type used by undertakers for picking up bodies was backed up to the door of Unit 14.

The plane made a circle. "Okay?" the pilot asked.

"Okay," Crowder said, and pointed to the east.

They flew for a few minutes out over the gleaming strip of highway.

"From here on," Mason said, "explore every road leading to the north."

"For how far?"

"Until you come to the end of it. It's only a few miles up to the other highway from El Centro and Holtville. We want to check the area in between."

"Can you tell me what you're looking for?" the pilot asked.

"Just property," Mason said.

The pilot brought the plane down to within a thousand

feet of the ground, explored one side road, then circled back toward the highway, started to explore another and said, "That *may* be what you *should* be looking for, up ahead."

Mason, in the copilot's seat, said, "I don't see anything."

The plane swept on, zoomed over the stalled car, climbed into a banking turn and came back.

"Apparently stuck in the sand," the pilot said. "That's the way it looks."

"Okay," Mason said, "fly north a couple of miles, then go back to the field. Stay with the plane when you get there. Have plenty of gas and be ready to take off the minute we show up."

"Okay," the pilot said, and climbed to a higher altitude as they started back for the field.

Mason turned to Crowder. "You can find that road all right?"

Crowder nodded.

"Is that near the property your client owns?" Mason asked Crowder.

"Right on it," Crowder said, turning toward Mason and closing one eye.

"I'd like to look at it from the ground," Mason said.

"I'll drive you out there," Crowder promised.

"Well, *that* didn't take long," the pilot said.

The plane was circling back over the field within a few minutes and settled down to a landing. The pilot taxied up to the rented car, turned the plane and stopped.

The passengers disembarked and approached the car.

When they were out of earshot of the pilot, Mason said to Crowder, "You'd better drive. You know the country. You know this road all right?"

"I know it," Crowder said. "It's up beyond the irrigated lands. It's a road that runs across to the Holtville Highway. There's hard-packed desert gravel for a way, and then sand for a spell."

"What do you mean, 'hard-packed desert gravel'?" Mason asked.

Crowder said, "We have winds down here—at times very violent winds. After thousands of years they've blown everything that's movable in the line of sand away from the surface. What's left is a hard-packed surface of sandworn gravel. Then when these winds slow down a bit, they start depositing sand. For that reason you'll find a lot of contrast down here; soil that's pure silt, sand hills and then hard-packed soil with little rocks that are polished smooth by sand and coated by the sunlight. I guess there's a chemical or something that gives the rocks kind of a dark, shiny surface on the part that's exposed to the sunlight."

"Hard to track in soil of that sort?" Mason asked.

"You can follow an automobile track, if it's fresh—if that's what you mean."

"That wasn't exactly what I meant," Mason said, "but we'll take a look. Get there as soon as possible. We're fighting time."

Crowder nodded, pressed the foot throttle and eased the car into speed.

"Now, I'm not certain about the ethics of this situation," Crowder said. "I'm leaving that entirely up to you."

"What do you mean, 'ethics'?"

"I take it," Crowder said, "we're going to discover evidence." ·

"Evidence of what?" Mason asked.

"I don't know," Crowder said.

"Neither do I," Mason told him. "We're inspecting physical facts."

"But what do we do with those facts? Do we— Well, suppose those facts should become evidence—at a later date?"

"That's exactly what I have in mind," Mason said. "We try to keep the date as much later as possible *if* the facts indicate that our client was emotionally disturbed."

"But if they're pertinent, what do we do?"

"If we *know* they're pertinent," Mason said, "we call the attention of the authorities to the facts."

"And you think they may be pertinent?"

"I'm afraid," Mason said, "they may be pertinent. However, as far as ethics are concerned, don't overlook the fact that a lawyer is ethically bound to protect his client. That's the first and foremost of all the rules of legal ethics.

"The people who formulate the canons of legal ethics take it for granted that an attorney will be protecting his client, so they lay down rules of professional conduct for the purpose of seeing the lawyer doesn't go too far. But the number one canon of ethics which should dominate all the others is that an attorney should be loyal to his client and should protect his client.

"Now then, we have a client who is hysterical. She is emotionally disturbed. She has told me a story which I can't repeat to the authorities because it's something she has told me as a professional confidence.

"If I can't tell it to the authorities in words without violating legal ethics, I can't very well tell the same story by actions."

"What do you mean?"

"If," Mason said, "the authorities knew that we took off in an automobile and came out here, the authorities would naturally assume that there was some reason for it and that our client had told us something that led us to take such an action."

"I see," Crowder said.

"Therefore," Mason said, "I see no reason for letting the authorities know that we drove out here looking for a car."

"I am beginning to understand," Crowder said, "why you were interested in looking over some property and the elaborate disinterest with which you regarded that car."

Mason said, "I think our pilot is fully trustworthy, but there's no use subjecting him to a practical test."

"And that's why you're anxious to have him get back to Los Angeles?" Crowder asked.

Mason grinned and said, "If he's not around here and doesn't hear about any murder case, he won't be doing any talking."

"Check," Crowder said.

Thereafter they were silent until Crowder made a left-hand turn.

"Is this the road?" Mason asked.

Crowder nodded.

"Let's take it slow and look for tracks."

"There's only a little traffic," Crowder said. "A few hunters come up in here. This road skirts some of those drifting sand hills I was telling you about. For some reason there's an eddy in the wind here, and as the wind, carrying sand, loses velocity, the sand spills out so to speak and starts forming drifting sand hills."

"This ground is hard packed," Mason said, "almost as if there were some kind of a cement binder."

"I think perhaps there is," Crowder said. "You can see those smooth pebbles all along here. They glisten in the sunlight."

The car sped along the road, then slowed as it went through a patch of sand, then speeded up again over another hard flat with pebbles reflecting the sunlight.

"There's the car up ahead," Crowder said. "Massachusetts license."

"I think we stop here," Mason said. "No, wait a minute. Go as far as you can without getting stuck."

"I can go pretty far," Crowder said, "because I was raised in this country. I know how to drive it. If you start fighting the sand, you get suck. If you just ease the wheels into motion and don't start churning the sand, you don't have any trouble. And if you do get into trouble, you can let some of the air out of your tires and—"

"That's it," Mason said. "Let's stop the car and let some air out of the tires. I don't want to leave any more tracks than necessary."

"All right," Crowder said, "we'll let a little air out of the tires and you'll be surprised what a difference it makes."

They stopped the car. Crowder took a match and depressed the valve stems, letting air out of the tires.

"We'll have to go pretty slow going back until we get to a service station," he said.

"That's all right," Mason told him.

"You want to tow that car out?" Crowder asked. "We could do it."

"We haven't a tow rope," Mason said.

"We can find some barbed wire around here somewhere," Crowder said. "Wrap it around several times and it makes a pretty good tow chain."

"I don't think we want to move the car," Mason said, "but there's no reason why we can't drive up until we find the road blocked by the car."

Crowder drove the car up to within five or six feet of the stalled automobile.

"You can see what happened," he said. "The driver tried to pour on the power . . . apparently trying to reverse . . . just churned up the sand and dug the car down into it."

Mason nodded, said to Crowder, "You and I are going to get out. Paul, you and Della sit inside. I don't want to leave any more tracks than necessary."

"There are tracks around here now," Crowder said. "Looks as though people had walked around here, and someone got out of the car on the left-hand side and didn't even bother to close the door. A light comes on automatically when that door is opened. In the course of time that will run down the battery. Think we should close the door?"

"I don't think so," Mason said. "We'd probably better leave things pretty much as we find them."

They approached the car, looked inside.

"Looking for blood or something?" Crowder asked.

"Something," Mason said.

He put a handkerchief over his hand, opened the rear door, looked inside, then suddenly straightened.

"What's that?" Crowder asked.

"That," Mason said, "is a green capsule lying on the driver's seat. From the size and appearance it may well be a barbiturate—one of the hypnotics."

"Sometimes used as a so-called 'truth serum' I understand," Crowder said.

"Injected hypodermically for a truth serum," Mason said, "so they can control the dosage— Now, what do you suppose *that's* doing here?"

"Think we should take it with us to find out what it is?" Crowder asked.

"We leave the capsule right where it is," Mason said, "but we take the keys out of the ignition and open the trunk."

The lawyer reached through the open door, extracted the keys from the ignition, selected the trunk key, walked back to the rear of the car, opened the trunk and looked inside.

"Nothing," Crowder said. "Is that what you expected?"

"I'm not expecting," Mason told him. "I'm looking and thinking."

Mason closed the trunk, put the ignition keys back in the lock, nodded to Crowder, and they returned to the rented automobile.

"That's all?" Crowder asked.

"That's all."

"What did you find?" Drake asked.

"Nothing that we could detect by a hurried superficial examination," Mason said, "but there was a green capsule on the driver's seat just to the right of where the driver would be sitting. The capsule could have been spilled from a woman's purse."

"And that's all you found?" Drake asked.

"That's all."

"And," Drake said, "you seem relieved."

"Well," Mason told him, "in a situation of this sort you never know what you might find in the car."

"You mean another corpse?" Drake asked.

Mason said, "I mean that you never know *what* you may find."

Crowder skillfully backed the car, then made a Y-turn in the soft sand, depressing the throttle just the right amount to put the power in the wheels without letting them slip or start churning up the sand.

They rode in silence back to the paved road.

They followed the pavement to the first service station, where Crowder had the tires inflated. While the attendant was putting in air, Mason went to the telephone booth and phoned the office of the sheriff.

When a voice answered saying, "Sheriff's office," Mason said, "I am an attorney from Los Angeles. I've been interested in some real estate in the valley and while making a flight in a chartered plane to look over the topography, I saw an automobile which apparently had been stuck in the sand and abandoned.

"This automobile is out on a road stretching from the Calexico-Yuma Highway north toward the Holtville-Yuma Highway. The turnoff is about fifteen miles east of Calexico. I would suggest you investigate.

"There was no sign of life, no one making any distress signals, so we didn't pay too much attention to it, but later on when I was making a more detailed inspection of the property and was out in the vicinity, we drove up to the car. It seems to be a car with a Massachusetts license number; it was stuck in the sand and abandoned. I thought you'd like to know about it."

"Thank you. We'll make a note of it," the officer said.

Mason hung up the phone, walked over to Duncan Crowder and said, "I'm leaving you on the job here. Paul Drake will stay here and help out. I've reported finding the car to the sheriff's office. You'll remember that we were looking at some property one of your clients had for sale."

"I'll remember," Duncan promised. "Anything else?"

"Nothing else," Mason said.

"Back to the airport?" Crowder asked.

Mason nodded, said, "I've given you a fee. Here's some money for expenses."

The lawyer opened his billfold, took out two one-hundred-dollar bills.

"Okay," Crowder said, "you have my telephone number. Keep in touch."

"And," Mason said, "you report to me on developments. Linda Calhoun will be showing up and making inquiries about her aunt. Linda is very friendly with George Latty. Anything Linda knows, she'll probably tell Latty. Anything Latty knows, he's damned apt to tell anyone.

"Paul, you keep this rented car, hang around here in Calexico, keep in touch with Crowder, and keep an ear to the ground—see what you can find out. Also put a shadow on Howland Brent. If he gets suspicious, tell the operative to drop him."

"What do I say in case I'm questioned—officially?" Drake asked.

Mason smiled and said, "You are making all of your reports to me, and I am, of course, co-operating with the authorities."

"Yes, I understand your co-operation," Drake said, running his forefinger in a cutting motion around his throat.

"Why, Paul," Mason told him, "I'm surprised! We're co-operating with the authorities. We've told them everything we've found."

"But you didn't tell them why you were looking for it."

"Certainly I did," Mason said. 'I told them that I was interested in buying some real property here. I am. It's a very fine investment. In fact I wouldn't be too surprised if I didn't actually take an option on some piece of property for thirty days or so."

"I see," Drake said dryly.

"And of course," Mason said, "now that you mention it, the fact that that car has a Massachusetts license *is* something of a coincidence, Paul."

When they were back at the airport Mason turned to Crowder and shook hands. "Stay on the job, Duncan," he said. "Telephone me just as soon as there are any developments. Paul Drake will keep in touch with you and he'll also keep in touch with me."

Crowder said, "I think I understand what you want, Mr. Mason."

"I'm quite satisfied you do," Mason said, grinning. "And I trust you are equally conversant with what I *don't* want."

"That, of course," Crowder said, "is a little more difficult but I think I have a general idea. I know that you're a very busy man and don't have time to fill me in on a lot of details. It's unfortunate as far as the authorities are concerned that you're in such a hurry to get back to your office in Los Angeles that we don't have time to sit down and talk things over."

"Indeed it is," Mason told him. "You'll have to use your judgment."

"I'll do my best," Crowder promised.

Mason took Della Street's arm, escorted her to the plane and helped her in. The pilot revved up the motors, and Duncan and Paul Drake waved good-by as the plane taxied down the field.

"Now there," Della Street said, "is a young attorney who should be going places."

Mason grinned. "He has what you can only describe as a good legal mind."

# Chapter 8

As Mason and Della Street entered the office, Gertie, the receptionist and switchboard operator, said, "Oh, Mr. Mason, Paul Drake is calling from Calexico. He wanted to get in touch with you just as soon as you came in. He said he would wait at the telephone. He expected you would be here about this time."

"All right," Mason said, "put the call through, Gertie, and see if we can get him."

Mason and Della Street went on into Mason's private office. Della Street started opening the mail with secretarial efficiency and was only halfway through the pile when the phone rang.

Mason nodded to Della Street to pick up her extension and heard Drake's voice on the line saying, "Hello, Perry."

"Okay," Mason said, "I'm on."

"This whole thing is a tempest in a teapot," Drake said. "The guy died a natural death."

"You're sure, Paul?"

"The coroner is. The guy just died a natural death—probably heart failure. There isn't any murder at all. Downright accommodating of him, I'd call it."

"You've advised Crowder?" Mason asked.

"Yes."

"Have you heard anything from Linda Calhoun?"

"Yes, she's down here. She must have arrived just about as you were taking off. She was at the motel when I got there."

"Did you tell her anything about Crowder?"

"Yes, I had Crowder with me and introduced him, and he

told her that he was working with you and took her to his office."

"What about George Latty?"

"He's disappeared somewhere. He checked out of the motel. I guess he's headed back for Los Angeles."

"And what about the abandoned car?"

"As nearly as I can tell," Drake said, "no one's doing anything about the car. They took your report and filed it. I don't think anyone's worried about it."

"What about Howland Brent, Paul?"

"He's moving heaven and earth trying to get Dr. Kettle to wake Lorraine up so he can talk with her. Dr. Kettle refuses. So Brent got in a rented car and took off. I have a man following him. He's probably headed back to Los Angeles."

Mason reached a quick decision. "All right, Paul, if it's a natural death there's no reason for the authorities to keep those motel units sealed up. Get busy and rent them before someone beats you to it. Tell the manager you're representing Lorraine Elmore and pay the rent in advance. Say she's lost the key. Get another key. Get in there and go over the place inch by inch.

"The coroner will want to remove the things from Dewitt's cabin. As soon as that has been done, you move in. Get a reservation on the place. Tell the manager I'm coming down to join you. Don't give her my name. Rent both units in your name."

"Okay," Drake said. "Can do."

"One other thing," Mason said, "rent that unit Latty moved out of. That will give us three in a row. Now, go through those units with a fine-toothed comb."

"What for, Perry? There hasn't been any murder and—"

"There's been a theft of over thirty-five thousand dollars," Mason interrupted. "We probably can't find where the money is, but we sure as hell can find out where it isn't."

"Okay," Drake promised. "I'll get busy."

"Right away," Mason said.

"*Right* away," Drake said, and hung up.

Mason and Della Street hung up simultaneously.

"Well?" Della Street asked.

Mason shook his head.

"Do we let it rest there if the authorities will?" she asked.

"Why not?"

"You have the story of a woman who says she saw him murdered."

"And," Mason said, "the body doesn't have a mark on it. There isn't any sign of violence and he died a natural death."

"Do *you* think he died a natural death?" she asked.

"I don't question the opinion of the authorities," Mason said. "See if you can get Duncan Crowder on the phone, Della."

Della Street relayed the call through to Gertie at the switchboard and a moment later nodded to Perry Mason. "He's coming on."

Mason picked up the phone and heard Duncan Crowder say, "Hello."

"Perry Mason, Duncan," the lawyer said. "How's everything coming at your end?"

"Everything's fine. The man died a natural death. I presume your detective told you?"

"That's right," Mason said. "What else do you know?"

"Not very much. Linda Calhoun is here in the office with me. We've been visiting and . . . well, sort of getting acquainted. Has George Latty been in touch with you?"

"No."

"He's apparently headed back to Los Angeles and will try to get in touch with you."

Mason said, "While you're talking with Linda, you might point out to her that all the physical evidence in this case indicates that her aunt has been emotionally upset. Now, I don't know what would cause this disturbance, but I would assume that it could be the use of barbiturates over a long period of time.

92

"She probably went to Montrose Dewitt's unit and tapped on the door and, when he didn't answer, opened the door to look in and saw him lying there on the floor dead. That was a very great emotional shock and she dashed into her unit, started tearing things to pieces, then jumped in her car and took a ride out in the desert.

"Now, I'm not a doctor but I assume that if a woman had taken a heavy dose of sedatives and then had experienced a shock like that and had started driving a car out into the desert with the subconscious realization in the back of her mind that a friend of whom she was very fond was dead, it might well be possible for her to have imagined this whole idea of a murder scene."

"I guess anything is possible," Crowder said. "We don't know very much about the workings of the human mind."

"It's a situation you might suggest to Dr. Kettle," Mason said.

"Now, wait a minute," Crowder told him. "Kettle will co-operate with us every way he can, but he wouldn't falsify a fact for anyone."

"This isn't a fact," Mason said. "It's a theory. You might point out to him that the indication is that Lorraine Elmore took a very heavy dose of barbiturates in order to sleep. She might have heard some noise—perhaps Dewitt called her name from the adjoining motel unit when he felt a heart attack coming on. She hurried to his side and he expired in her arms. That could have triggered a whole set of ideas."

"I get it," Crowder said. "I got it the first time, but I'm just pointing out to you, Mr. Mason, that Dr. Kettle won't go for it unless it's medically sound."

Mason said, "*I* think it's medically sound. You might talk with Linda along those lines."

"I'll talk with her," Crowder said. "She seems very intelligent."

"I'm satisfied you both are," Mason told him, and hung up.

The lawyer had no sooner replaced the phone than Della

Street's phone rang and she picked up the instrument, said, "Yes, Gertie," then said, "Just a minute."

She turned to Mason and said, "Belle Freeman is in the office. She'd like to see you."

"Belle Freeman?" Mason asked. "That's the one that knew Dewitt and took out the marriage license with him?"

Della Street nodded.

"I think we want to see her," Mason said, "but this case certainly is taking some puzzling turns. Go get her and bring her in, Della. Let's see what she has to say."

Della nodded, went to the reception room and returned with a woman in her mid-thirties, a woman who had the figure of a woman in her twenties. Her blue eyes sparkled, her step was full of bounce.

"Mr. Mason," she said, "I *know* this is an imposition, but I talked with Linda Calhoun last night and somehow I feel that I know you and I think perhaps you can help me."

"Well, now wait a minute," Mason said. "In the first place I'm glad you came in. I had been thinking about getting in touch with you; however, *I* can't help *you*. This is a case in which I already have a client. I wouldn't want to even consider representing anyone whose interests might be in conflict. . . ."

"But they're not in conflict," she said. "All I want is my money back, and I have a boy friend in El Centro who will help."

"Well, that might—it just might—be in conflict," Mason said. "But with the understanding that anything you tell me is not in confidence and that I can't represent you as long as there is any possibility of a conflict, I'd certainly be glad to talk with you, because you have some information that I want."

"What, Mr. Mason?"

"I would like to know a great deal about Montrose Dewitt."

"The man's a heel, a fourflusher, a phony from way back."

"I can understand all that," Mason said. "I'm not talking about his character. I'm talking about his background."

"I don't know too much about his background, but I know everything about his character, and I hope you can send him to jail. That's what I came to see you about. I wanted—"

"You can't send him to jail," Mason interrupted.

"You can't?" she asked, her face showing her evident disappointment. "Now that you've found him why can't—"

Mason shook his head. "He's dead."

"What!"

"He's dead. He died last night in Calexico."

"How— Why— How did it happen?"

"Apparently he just died in his sleep," Mason said.

She started to say something, then caught herself.

Mason raised his eyebrows.

"I'm sorry," she said. "I make it a rule never to speak ill of the dead. I didn't know."

"Well, that isn't going to keep you from telling me something that would give me a clue as to his past."

She said, "I'm not going to be able to help you there very much, Mr. Mason. The man had the most mysterious personality and background—he simply vanished."

"He defrauded you out of some money?"

"All of my savings."

"How much?"

"It was more than the figure I've admitted. There was an inheritance and he got away with everything."

"You went to the police?"

"No, I didn't, Mr. Mason. I— There were reasons. I couldn't afford publicity. I suppose this is all an old story to you, but I was a babe in the woods. I walked in like a sheep to the slaughter. He told me we were going to pool our assets and that he was going to raise some more money from his friends. He had a sure-fire opportunity to make millions and all it needed was a little capital."

"A convincing talker?" Mason asked.

"He convinced me."

"By talk?"

"Well, he had what you would call a skillful approach. He knew how to flatter a woman and make her feel important and . . . well, I fell for it."

"How did you meet him?"

"Through correspondence. I wrote a letter of protest to a newspaper. The newspaper published it. It didn't publish my address, of course, but he found out my address—that wouldn't have been too difficult. I was a registered voter. He wrote me a letter telling me how smart I was, how well I had expressed my ideas, how much they meant to him and how refreshing it was to encounter a person of such intelligence and perspicacity in the readers' column of the paper.

"Well, of course I fell for it. His address was on the upper left-hand corner of the envelope, and I wrote him a brief note thanking him, and then he wrote me enclosing a newspaper clipping that he thought would be interesting to me, and the first thing I knew we were meeting, having dinner dates, and then . . . well, then he just went ahead with a whirlwind campaign."

"But what did he tell you about himself?" Mason asked. "What did he say he was doing?"

"He wasn't doing anything. He had just returned from Mexico. He had been engaged in some activities there which he said were classified and he couldn't talk about them, but he had had many adventures. He was the dashing soldier-of-fortune type."

"How long did he say he'd been in Mexico?"

"He said he'd been there for more than a year—but you know there's something funny, Mr. Mason. The man couldn't speak Spanish."

"No?"

"I don't think he knew more than a dozen words of Spanish. He told all about his adventures, and then I introduced him to a friend who could speak Spanish and mentioned something about Montrose having been in Mexico, and the friend started speaking Spanish to him."

96

"What happened?"

"Montrose stopped the man, said that he had never bothered to learn Spanish because he felt that it put him at a disadvantage; that it was always better to have an interpreter and work through the interpreter."

"And you were taken in by that explanation?"

"At the time, yes. I'd have been taken in by anything he did."

"And then, after the man got your money, what happened?"

"We were to be married, but he just never showed up, that's all. He simply vanished."

"No word from him, no explanation?"

"Nothing," she said, her lips tightening. "If you could ever realize the way I felt when it began to dawn on me. . . . First there was that awful period of anxiety, feeling that he'd been hurt in an automobile accident, or something; then an attempt to trace him, and gradually the sickening realization that I'd been played for a fool."

"And you did nothing about it?"

"I tried to find him."

"How?"

"I hired a private detective until I realized that was throwing good money after bad."

"And the detective couldn't find him?"

She shook her head. "Not a trace."

"The detective made reports?"

"Oh, yes, he made copious reports telling me what he'd done. He referred to Montrose as the subject, and the reports were skillfully designed to show me that I was getting a run for my money. That's all I was getting, a run for my money."

Mason said, "By any chance do you have those reports? Did you save them?"

"I have them here," she said. "I came prepared to do everything I could to help Linda and . . . well, I wanted to do something to get even with Montrose Dewitt."

97

She opened her purse, took out an envelope and handed it to Mason.

"May I keep these reports for a while?" Mason asked.

"Keep them forever, if you want," she said. "I don't know why I was saving them. They're just a memory of a headache."

Mason said, "The man must have had some hide-out where he could vanish—probably some other city where he carried on his activities. Perhaps he worked several cities at the same time. It's unusual for a man to keep the same name and then to vanish completely."

"That's what I thought," she said, "but I felt that I was throwing good money after bad and, as a friend pointed out to me, there wasn't very much I could do if I did catch up with him except— Well, I didn't want to try to prosecute him for obtaining money under false pretenses, or anything of that sort.

"In fact, Mr. Mason, I don't know that there were any false pretenses. I simply trustingly turned over my money to him to invest. We were going to be partners in life and all that sort of stuff—and I went completely overboard.

"I guess with your experience and legal background you can just about put the whole story together. I was a fool."

"You'd been married?" Mason asked.

She shook her head. "I was a bachelor girl. I had been very much in love, and the man I loved had been killed. I was true to his memory for quite a while. Then things began to happen. I drifted into an attachment and that didn't pan out, and the first thing I knew I was no longer a young woman and I tried to pretend I didn't care. I was a bachelor girl. I was going to live my own life beholden to no one. Women aren't made to do that, Mr. Mason. They want someone to work for, someone to love, someone to cherish and, if you come right down to it, someone to obey.

"Then along came Montrose Dewitt with this dashing devil-may-care air of his and I was just like putty."

"Did he have an automobile?" Mason asked.

"Yes, it's all in those reports. The detective traced the ownership of the automobile and all of that.

"You'll find that there's no record of Montrose Dewitt ever paying income taxes, ever having a social security number, but he did have a driving license."

"And you were living here in Los Angeles at the time?"

"No, Mr. Mason, I was living in Ventura, working there. And Montrose Dewitt had an apartment in Hollywood. The job I had was ... well, if there had been any scandal connected with my name— Well, I just had to grit my teeth and start all over again. I just couldn't afford the publicity, and I can't very well afford it now. That's one of the reasons I came up here to see you, Mr. Mason. I would dislike very much to have Linda Calhoun say anything that would involve me.

"I tried to reach her this morning but couldn't get her and I knew you were representing her, so I thought I'd come to you and give you what help I could and ask you to protect me as much as possible—I mean from publicity."

"Thanks a lot," Mason told her. "If you'll let me study those reports I may be able to learn something from them, and I certainly appreciate the fact that you have told me this much."

She gave him her hand, said, "I've tried to make it a closed chapter in my life but it keeps cropping up. I feel better now that I've told you the whole story and given you those reports. I was hoping they might be of some help."

"I'll study them," Mason promised as Della Street escorted Belle Freeman to the exit door.

"Well?" Mason asked, when the door closed.

Della Street shook her head. "The man certainly seemed to have a way with women."

"And," Mason said, "what the police refer to as a *modus operandi*. He'd make his initial contact through the mails. That means he must have written quite a few letters to different people. He couldn't have picked live prospects every time just by taking the names of persons who had written letters that were published. There must have been times when the women who wrote those letters were married, or didn't have any money, or did have boy friends who wouldn't have meekly surrendered their women to some character who had a dashing manner, a black eye patch, and a mysterious background."

"That's right," Della Street said.

"In other words," Mason said, "the man must have written dozens of letters. When he'd get a reply he'd start checking. If he found the party had some money, then he would follow up."

"Will that help us?" she asked.

"It may give us a little help on his background," Mason said. "It probably won't help otherwise because we already knew how he worked. I was merely pointing out the problems which he faced as a confidence man. The thing that is puzzling is the manner in which he could completely disappear.

"You would have thought that a man who was engaging in a confidence game wouldn't have had the temerity to use such a distinctive means of identification as the black eye patch."

"That probably made him distinctive and more dashing and more attractive," Della Street said.

"But a thousand times more conspicuous," Mason said, "and . . ."

Suddenly he stopped.

"What?" she asked.

Mason snapped his fingers and said, "Of course! I should have thought of it before."

"What?"

"He wore the eye patch because he wanted to be conspicuous. He only put on his eye patch when he was going to make a swindle. Then when he disappeared he simply took off the eye patch and substituted a glass eye. Then he could fade into the background and blend with thousands of other individuals.

"No one would ever think of looking for him except as the man with the black eye patch."

"*That* certainly sounds logical," Della Street said.

Maxon, suddenly excited, said, "Let's get hold of Paul Drake, Della. I want him to get a colored sketch of Montrose Dewitt's remaining eye. Then we'll get in touch with people who manufacture glass eyes. There aren't many of them—it's quite a specialty—"

Mason was interrupted by the telephone ringing a succession of short bells, a signal always used by Gertie at the switchboard when there was some emergency, or when she was excited.

Della Street picked up the telephone, said, "Yes," then said to Mason, "It's Paul Drake on the line. He's excited."

Mason picked up the telephone, said, "Hello, Paul. What is it?"

"There's hell to pay down here," Drake said.

"How come?"

"Montrose Dewitt left a pint whiskey flask in his suitcase," Drake said. "One of the boys from the coroner's office took a nip, just to have a drink on the dead man. It was pretty good whiskey and he felt it shouldn't be wasted."

"What happened?" Mason asked.

"The guy's in the care of a physician right now," Drake said. "The whiskey was loaded to the gills with some powerful drug, probably one of the barbiturates.

"That puts an entirely different aspect on the whole case and makes it look like murder after all. They're going to analyze the contents of Dewitt's stomach and send the vital organs to a laboratory to be tested for barbiturates. I thought I'd let you know."

"Does Crowder know?" Mason asked.

"He knows."

"Linda?"

"I understand Crowder is getting in touch with her."

"All right," Mason said, "here's what I want you to do, Paul. Get the coroner to let you make a colored sketch of the man's single eye. Get an artist with some colored crayons and make a sketch of the coloring of that eye. I want all of those little islands of coloring that you find in the eye, the most accurate chart you can make."

"Then what?" Drake asked.

"Then," Mason said, "I want you to get back here as fast as you can and start covering people who make glass eyes. I want to see if we can find whoever it was who made the glass eye for Montrose Dewitt."

"But he didn't have a glass eye, Perry. He wore the patch all the time and—"

"And then when he disappeared," Mason interrupted, "he simply put the patch in the bottom of a bureau drawer, put the glass eye in and very probably assumed another identity.

"You'll remember the significant fact that while he was supposed to be a traveling man his automobile showed only a very low mileage. Put all that stuff together, Paul, and it means that Montrose Dewitt had another identity somewhere pretty near Los Angeles.

"Now, if that happened, two men are missing and there's only one corpse. I want you to get busy and check on all missing persons. I want you to check on that glass eye. You better get back here and start putting men to work."

"Well," Drake said thoughtfully, "that's sure an angle, Perry. I'll be seeing you."

"Has the sheriff done anything about that car yet?"

"That report you made," Drake said, "is probably buried in the files."

"Okay," Mason told him, "we've got some time yet before Lorraine Elmore comes out from under her sedation. We probably don't have that much time before the police start checking on her car and then appreciate the significance of the report I made.

"We've got to be well ahead of them by that time, because this development of the drugged whiskey means that someone is going to be charged with murder and it may well be our client."

"Oh-oh," Drake said, and then after a moment added, "I see your point, Perry. I'll get up there right away."

# Chapter 9

It was midafternoon when Paul Drake's code knock sounded on the door of Mason's private office.

Della Street opened the door and said, "You got back in a hurry, Paul."

"I was told to. I caught a plane out of Imperial via Palm Springs."

"Anything new, Paul?" Mason asked.

"Quite a bit of it," Drake said, "but I can't unscramble it."

"What is it?"

"Well, in the first place, Perry, I'm afraid I started something when I got the coroner to let me make a color sketch of the dead man's eye."

"What happened?"

"There was an artist down there who really had a lot of talent and she was perfectly willing to make a color sketch of a dead eye.

"However, it's a small community, and the coroner thought that was a story that was good enough for the newspapers. He's going to run for office so he wanted newspaper support, and he let the cat out of the bag."

"What else?"

"Well, that's about the story, Perry. I got in an hour ago, passed the color sketch on to one of my best operatives and started him covering the persons who make glass eyes to order.

"That's quite a profession, Perry. It's an art to make a really good artificial eye with all the natural coloring."

Mason nodded.

The phone rang.

Della Street picked up the instrument, said, "Hello," then nodded to Paul Drake. "For you, Paul."

Drake went over to the instrument, said, "Hello," then after listening for a moment said, "All right, what's the address?"

The detective made a notation on a pad of paper, said, "He's sure?"

"That's right."

"And what's that name? Hale? H-a-l-e. Okay, what's the first name? Spell it. W-e-s-t-o-n. Okay, that's all you can do at that end. We'll check on it."

Cradling the phone and turning to Mason, Drake said, "Well, we seem to be getting somewhere, Perry. My operative located a Selwig Hedrick, who is one of the top experts in the business, and he recognized the eye immediately: said that he had made it for a man named Weston Hale. The address is the Roxley Apartments."

Mason said, "It's a good even-money bet that Weston Hale will turn up missing tonight and no one will be sure where he is or what happened to him."

"In other words, Weston Hale and Montrose Dewitt are one and the same?" Drake asked.

Mason nodded.

The telephone rang and Della Street picked up the instrument, said, "Hello," then gestured to Mason. "Duncan Crowder calling from Calexico," she said.

Mason picked up his telephone, said, "Hello . . . yes, this is Perry Mason . . . hello, Duncan, what's new?"

Crowder said, "I hate to bring you bad news, Mr. Mason, but I guess that's what it is."

"What is it?"

"For some reason the authorities suddenly woke up to the significance of the report you made on the car out in the middle of the desert with the Massachusetts license. They sent a tow car out, snaked the car out of the sand, and have brought it in for investigation. There was a capsule of Somniferal on the front seat, and in the cabin that was occupied by Lorraine Elmore they found a bottle which had contained Somniferal capsules. The bottle was a large one with a capacity for a hundred capsules and is so labeled."

"Prescription?" Mason asked.

"Yes. It was a prescription. It seems our client has been emotionally disturbed. A doctor has been prescribing for her. She told him she was taking a long trip and wanted enough sleeping medicine to last her. He gave her the prescription.

"The sheriff talked with him on the phone. He said Mrs. Elmore's trouble was such that if she started worrying about not having enough sleeping medicine along it would have been the worst thing possible. He said she only takes a capsule when she becomes disturbed, that she averages about eight to twelve capsules a month but if she felt she didn't have enough to last her she'd become so upset her nervous trouble would be greatly exaggerated.

"Naturally they're now very anxious to get Mrs. Elmore's story, and particularly they want to know how the Somniferal from her bottle got into Montrose Dewitt's stomach."

"They can't prove it's the *same* Somniferal," Mason said.

"Perhaps not, but they're certainly acting on that assumption. Dr. Kettle is standing firm. His client is under sedation and he says any statement that she might make at the present time would reasonably be expected to be inaccurate, and perhaps the facts might be all mixed up with imaginative memories from the dream world. He's expressed it rather strongly and quite vividly."

Mason thought for a moment, then said, "All right, Duncan, let Dr. Kettle emphasize the fact that any statement she might make is very apt to be inaccurate, colored by imaginative facts from a world of fantasy, and completely unreliable; but if they want to accept the responsibility of a statement being made under those circumstances he'll let them talk with the patient as soon as she wakes up."

Crowder said, "They'll grab that offer. They're tremendously anxious right now to find out what this is all about, how the car got out there, what the connection is between

Dewitt and Mrs. Elmore, and when she saw him last and all that. Should Dr. Kettle waken her now?"

"No. Wait until she wakes up. Tip Dr. Kettle off to play it up strong, that any statement she may make will be very apt to be inaccurate, and then when she wakes up let her make that statement."

"You know what they'll do then," Crowder said. "They'll take her into custody and later on when she is in full possession of her faculties they'll play the tape recording of that statement back to her and ask her how much is true and how much of it isn't true."

"And by that time," Mason said, "we will have advised her to say nothing to anyone.

"Keep in touch with the situation. The minute she makes a statement you notify me. Then I express great indignation over the telephone that any such advantage should be taken of a client. I state that under the circumstances I am advising her not to make any more statements under any circumstances, except in the presence of both of her attorneys."

"And she dries up like a clam?"

"Like a clam," Mason said.

"Think she'll do it?"

"She will if you talk with her in the right way."

"What's the right way?" Crowder asked.

"Scare the pants off her," Mason said.

"Okay," Crowder told him, "will do."

"We're working on a new angle up here," Mason said. "Play that one down there in just exactly that way and get her to clam up immediately after she's told that story."

"That's the way it'll be done," Crowder said, and hung up.

# Chapter 10

"We check on Weston Hale?" Drake asked after Mason had returned the receiver to its cradle.

Mason nodded. "This is one case where we're keeping just one jump ahead of the police, Paul, instead of being two jumps behind. It's a wonderful sensation."

Drake said, "I'm thinking of what the sensation is going to be when they do catch up with us."

"We're not violating any law," Mason said. "We're not concealing any evidence. We're simply checking. Anyone has a right to do that."

"I know, I know," Drake said, "but I'm worried about it just the same."

"Anyway," Mason pointed out, "there won't be any Weston Hale. We'll find that he's disappeared."

"Do you want me along?" Della Street asked.

Mason thought for a moment, then said, "No, Della. You stay here and tend the store. We're just running down a blind alley, but in order to prove our point we have to determine that it is a blind alley. Come on, Paul, let's go."

The Roxley Apartments proved to be a six-story apartment house of the better class. The directory showed that Weston Hale's apartment was 522.

"We may as well go up," Mason said, "and knock on the door. Then we'll hunt up the manager and see what we can find out."

They went up in the elevator, walked down to the apartment and pressed the mother-of-pearl button.

Chimes sounded on the inside, then lapsed into silence.

"Do it about three times," Mason said. "We just want to make sure there's no answer."

Drake nodded, pressed the button again.

Almost instantly the door opened. A man with a robe around him, his eyes swollen, his nose red, said in a voice so thick it was hard to understand, "Whaddyuh wand?"

"Are you Mr. Hale?" Mason asked.

The man shook his head. "Hale ain't here. Whaddyuh wand with Hale?"

"We wanted to talk with him," Mason said. "Does he live here?"

"Hale and I share the apardmend. I gotta cold—gettin' the flu, I think. You guys gonna get the flu if you stick around. Come back later."

"Where is Mr. Hale?" Mason asked.

"On the job—working."

"Where?"

"Investors' Mortgage & Refinancing Company."

"Where's it located?"

"West Bemont Street. Whaddyuh wand with him? Who are you?"

"Mr. Hale has a glass eye?" Mason asked.

"A what?"

"A glass eye."

"News to me," the man said. "Always looked all right to me. Whaddyuh wand? Who are you?"

"What's *your* name?" Mason asked.

"Ronley Andover. Now look, I've got a fever and I've been in bed for a coupla days, fighting this thing. I'm standing in a draft right now. Why don't you guys go home before you get the flu?"

"We'll come in," Mason said. "We'll only be a minute."

"If you're coming in, you're going to talk to me in bed. I've got a fever and I'm supposed to stay in bed and keep covered up, drink lots of fruit juices, a little whiskey, and take a lot of aspirin. Now, if you fellows want to take a chance on the flu, come on in."

Drake looked dubious but Mason said, "We'll take a chance."

They entered the apartment.

"This is a double apartment?" Mason asked.

"That's right. Hale's room is over there. He has his own bath. My bedroom is over there. I have my own bath. We use this as a sitting room and there's a kitchen in back. Now, I can't tell you fellows anything about Hale except he's on the job. Go see him there. I'm going to bed. I feel lousy."

The man went into the bedroom, jumped into bed with the robe still around him, shivered slightly, produced an inhaler, took a long sniff, sneezed, and regarded them with watery eyes.

Mason said, "We're trying to find out all we can about Weston Hale. It's very important."

"What's important about it?" Andover asked.

Mason hurried on without answering the question. "I'm an attorney and this man is a detective."

"Police or private?"

"Private."

"What do you want?"

"We want to find out about Hale."

"Why not go ask him?"

"We will as soon as we leave here."

"Go ahead and leave, then. No one's holding you."

"We are going to go and see Hale," Mason said, "but first we'd like to find out if he is the specific person in whom we are interested. May we look in his room?"

"Sure, why not? . . . No, now, wait a minute— Hell, no! I don't feel right or I wouldn't have said yes in the first place— Of course you can't look in his room. That's his. I don't know what he's got in there. I'm not going to let a couple of strangers go prowling around in there."

"Could you come to the door with us—just open the door and let us just look inside without touching anything?"

"What are you looking for?"

"We want to try and get a line on him."

"Why?"

"We have a matter of considerable importance to take up with him," Mason said.

"You can't take it up with him by looking in his room," Andover said. "I don't think he'd like it that way. I wouldn't like it that way, and I'm not gonna get out of bed. I feel like hell and if you guys get the bug I've got, you're gonna wish to hell you'd never heard of Weston Hale."

"How long has he been sharing the apartment with you?" Mason asked.

"I don't know. Four or five months. I had another fellow here. He got transferred. . . . I'd rather have somebody sharing the apartmend with me and have a big apartmend than be cooped up in one of these little singles. . . . What's all the urgency about Weston Hale?"

"We're just trying to reach him," Mason said. "Tell me, did you ever know him to wear a black patch over his bad eye?"

"I tell you, I didn't know he had a bad eye. The guy seems to see all right."

Mason asked, "Does he have a portable typewriter?"

"He sure does."

"Doing some writing?"

"Lots of it. He keeps pounding that typewriter, when he's home, into the small hours. He's a worker, that guy."

Mason said, "We think a friend of his, Montrose Dewitt, is in trouble and we'd like to talk to Hale about him. Did you ever hear him mention Montrose Dewitt?"

The man on the bed rolled his head from side to side in a gesture of negation.

"Never heard him mention Montrose Dewitt?"

"No, I told you."

Mason said, "We'll come back when you're feeling better, Andover."

"What's all the excitement about? What about Dewitt?"

Mason said, "We think he was murdered in Calexico sometime last night."

"Murdered!"

"That's right."

"Well, whaddyuh know?" Andover said.

110

"Under those circumstances, may we look in Hale's room?" Mason inquired.

"Under *those* circumstances, you can just get the hell out of here until you come back with a police officer."

Andover turned over in bed, coughed, pulled the blanket up over him and said, "Now I'm warning you, don't go prowling around on the way out. Just beat it."

"We thank you for your co-operation, Mr. Andover," Mason said. "I'm sorry you're not feeling well and I'm sorry you don't appreciate our position."

"Well, you guys just quit worrying about that," Andover said. "It doesn't make any difference whether *I* appreciate *your* position, I sure as hell appreciate mine and nobody's going in there until somebody shows up who has the authority to go in there."

Mason nodded to Drake, said, "Well, thanks a lot, Andover."

"Don't mention it," Andover said sarcastically.

Mason and Drake left the bedroom, paused momentarily in the sitting room. Drake looked toward the door on the other side. Mason shook his head, opened the door into the corridor. "Good-by, Andover," he called.

There was no answer from the bedroom.

"He wrote letters," Mason said. "There must have been a lot of replies. The man must have had a lot of nibbles before he'd be ready to sink his hook in the fish he wanted. It might help a lot if we could find some of those letters."

"That wouldn't give any indication of who killed him," Drake said.

Mason's eyes were level-lidded with concentration. "It would show what a heel he was and how he made his living. Lots of times in a murder case, Paul, it pays to show that the corpse was a rat and that whoever killed him was a public benefactor."

"So now we go see Hale?"

"Now we go see what excuse Hale has made for not being available. Hale's dead."

## Chapter 11

Henry T. Jasper, president of the Investors' Mortgage & Refinancing Company, said, "This is really an honor, Mr. Mason. I've heard a lot about you, and I'm familiar with some of your more spectacular cases.

"And this is Paul Drake of the Drake Detective Agency?

"I assume, gentlemen, that you would not be calling upon me at this late hour in the afternoon unless it was on a matter of some major importance."

"I don't know," Mason said. "Frankly, I am puzzled and we're trying to get information."

"And perhaps I can assist you?"

"I think you can. What can you tell us about Weston Hale?"

"Not very much," Jasper said, smiling, "because there's not very much to tell. Hale is one of those quiet, retiring personalities who revels in detail. He is one of our most trusted employees, has been with us for a period of some seven years, and is invaluable to the business."

"Would it be possible for us to talk with him?" Mason asked.

"Why, certainly," Jasper said.

"Now?"

"Come, come, gentlemen. It's after our closing hours. I was working here on a matter of some importance and of course some of the clerical staff are here but ... well, I assume Mr. Hale has gone home. Just a moment, I'll find out."

Jasper pressed a button on his desk and a few moments later a rather tired-looking woman in her early forties opened the door and said, "Yes, Mr. Jasper?"

"Is Hale here?"

"No, sir."

"He's gone home?"

"He wasn't here today."

"Oh, he wasn't?"

She shook her head. "He was going to make some appraisals up in Santa Barbara. You remember you asked him about a survey of the physical assets supporting the bond issue in that subdivision?"

"Oh, that's right," Jasper said. "I *did* want him to go over that. We discussed it a few days ago and he said he'd go up there just as soon as he could get some things cleaned up here."

"Do you know where we could reach him?" Mason asked Jasper.

Jasper in turn relayed the inquiry on to the woman standing in the doorway by raising his eyebrows.

She shook her head. "Just in Santa Barbara. He probably is staying at a motel. I think he drove up."

"May I ask you why you're interested, Mr. Mason?" Jasper inquired.

"It's a question of identity," Mason said. "Could you tell me, does Mr. Hale have an artificial eye?"

Jasper smiled and shook his head. "No, he has both eyes and . . ." Suddenly he broke off at something he saw on the face of the woman in the doorway. "What is it, Miss Selma?" he asked.

"I've sometimes wondered," she said. "Have you ever noticed, Mr. Jasper, whenever Mr. Hale looks at anything he turns his head. You never see him turning his eyes. He will sit in a conversation with two or more people, will listen to one, then gravely turn his head to face the other when he wants to hear what that person has to say.

"I've noticed it for some time. At first I thought he was deaf and was resorting to lip reading but more recently I've been puzzled. I've been wondering why he did it. The explanation of an artificial eye has never occurred to me, but

113

now that the thought has been suggested I think perhaps that may be the explanation."

"Is he married?" Mason asked.

Jasper was the one who answered the question. "No, he is not. I think the man virtually lives for his work. He spends many of his evenings here. Hale has a great mind for detail and he makes it a point to keep a check on the background of most of the companies issuing securities in which we are interested from a standpoint of investment."

Mason glanced at Paul Drake. "I guess that covers it," he said. "I would like very much to get in touch with Mr. Hale. If he should phone in, will you ask him to please give me a ring?"

"Oh, he'll be in tomorrow," Jasper said. "That is, I assume he will, unless something in that Santa Barbara situation is more complicated than would appear on the surface."

"That's an unusual situation?" Mason asked.

"Well, in a way, yes. We have invested some money in securities issued by a corporation engaged in subdivision work. The securities represent improvement bonds and recently there has been some question— You'll have to pardon me, I'm afraid, Mr. Mason. I don't think I care to go into it at this time, particularly in advance of a report from Hale."

"Hale is fully qualified to check into a matter of that sort?" Mason asked.

Jasper smiled and said, "Hale is the greatest little ferret you ever saw. He'll nose into a situation, worm his way through masses of detail and has an uncanny instinct for getting to the heart of the matter. . . . That's all, Miss Selma, thank you. I just wanted to see if Mr. Hale was in the office."

She smiled and withdrew.

"Well," Mason said, "I guess that pretty much covers the situation."

"I'll be glad to have Mr. Hale get in touch with you," Jasper said. And then added with a note of curiosity in his

114

voice, "I assume that the fact you came here personally, Mr. Mason, means that you want to see him about something that is rather out of the ordinary."

"Yes, I think perhaps it is," Mason said. "By the way, did Hale have any brothers—a twin brother, perhaps?"

"Not that I know of. I have never heard him mention any relatives. He— Did you say, *did* he have, Mr. Mason?"

Mason nodded.

"You're using the past tense?"

Mason said, "There is a possibility that a man who died in a motel at Calexico last night might have been related to Hale."

"Oh," Jasper said. "He doesn't have any relatives, at least in this part of the country. I'm quite certain of that, and if there'd been a brother I— But you used the past tense in regard to Mr. Hale himself."

"That's right," Mason said. "In the event the corpse isn't Hale's twin brother there's a very good possibility the corpse is that of Weston Hale."

"What!" Jasper exclaimed incredulously.

"I'm simply mentioning possibilities," Mason said. "I'm not prepared to make any statement to that effect, and my visit here is purely in the nature of a search for information."

"Why . . . why— You must have *some* grounds for your assumption, Mr. Mason."

"I wish I did have," Mason said. "At the present time I'm simply following a trail. Do you know if Hale is related in any way to a Montrose Dewitt?"

"Dewitt . . . Dewitt," Jasper said. "The name has a familiar ring somehow, but I can't seem to place it specifically."

"Well, no matter," Mason said. "The situation will doubtless be cleared up after I've had a chance to talk with Mr. Hale tomorrow. Thank you very much, Mr. Jasper."

Drake and Mason shook hands with Jasper and left the office, leaving the president of the company standing by his desk, a look of perplexity on his face.

"Well," Mason said, as they left the building, "it looks very much as though we're headed in the right direction."

"In the right direction, but how far are we going?" Drake asked.

"To the end of the trail," Mason said.

Drake was pessimistic. "It looks as if it might be a blind alley," he said.

Mason might not have heard him. His face was a mask of concentration. He drove to his office building without speaking more than a dozen words.

As they left the elevator and Drake opened the door of his office, Mason paused for a moment in the doorway. "I want to keep in touch with you, Paul, and—"

Drake's switchboard operator said, "Oh, Mr. Mason, I have a message for you."

Mason moved on into the office.

"Miss Street telephoned on the unlisted phone," the operator said, "and asked that you call her before you go down the hall to your office."

Mason raised his eyebrows. "No idea what it is?"

"No," she said. "Something important."

"All right," Mason said, "get her on the line. What phone can I take?"

"That one on the desk," she said.

Drake said, "The probabilities are, Perry, that there's an official delegation waiting for you in your office and Della wants to tip you off."

Mason shook his head. "If the police were in the office, Paul, they wouldn't give Della a chance to get to the telephone to tip me off."

The switchboard operator put through the call and nodded to Mason.

Mason said, "Hello, Della."

Della, her voice low, said, "You have company, Chief. I thought you might like to know before you reach the office."

"Who?" Mason asked.

"One of them," she said, "is your friend, George Latty."

"And the other?" Mason asked.

"The other is Baldwin L. Marshall, the district attorney of Imperial County."

"That," Mason said, "is a strange combination. Do they seem antagonistic or otherwise?"

"It's a little hard to state," Della said, "but I think it's otherwise. Latty has a chip on his shoulder, but I would gather he had reached some sort of an understanding with the district attorney and that's the reason I thought you should be tipped off."

"What sort of a fellow is the district attorney?" Mason asked.

"In his middle thirties, very alert; reddish hair, blue eyes and a quick, nervous manner. He's very aggressive."

"How tall?"

"Around five feet eleven; rather slender; nervous and tense and . . . well, dangerous, if you know what I mean."

"I know what you mean," Mason said. "I'll come to the office in a few minutes. . . . I take it that the district attorney of Imperial County is just a little hostile?"

"Well," Della Street said, "he's being very, very official."

Mason said, "Latty has told him something—the question is what, and how much? All right, Della. Don't let on that I've been tipped off. I'll be there in a minute or two. Where are these people?"

"I put them in the law library. I didn't want to leave them in the reception room."

"And where are you talking from?"

"From the phone behind Gertie's desk at the switchboard."

"All right," Mason said, "go into the private office, leave the door to the law library open—"

"It's already open," she said. "They left it open."

"All right, that's fine. I'll come in from the hall door. As soon as I open the door you can start with the act."

"What sort of an act?"

"Just ad lib," Mason said. "Follow my lead."

Mason hung up the telephone, turned to Paul Drake, nar-

117

rowed his eyes thoughtfully and said, "Now, just what could George Latty have told the district attorney of Imperial County that would turn the heat on me?"

"Well," Drake said dryly, "he *could* have told him the truth."

Mason smiled. "The question is, how much of the truth?"

"How much truth could you stand?" Drake asked.

Mason grinned by way of answer, said, "Well, I guess I'll go down and see what it's all about, Paul."

"Want me along?" Drake asked.

Mason shook his head. "Just keep on the job, Paul. Keep operatives on Howland Brent, and just for good measure you'd better put a tail on George Latty when he leaves the office. That young man is getting just a little too ubiquitous to suit me."

Mason left the detective's office, walked down the corridor to his own office, fitted his latchkey to the door marked PERRY MASON—*Private* and opened the door.

Della Street was standing by the lawyer's desk sorting mail.

"Hello, Della," Mason said. "It's time to go home. What's new, anything?"

Della Street said, "You have a couple of visitors, Mr. Mason. Mr. Baldwin Marshall and Mr. George Latty."

"Latty, huh?" Mason said. "That guy certainly gets around. What's he want, and who's Marshall?"

"Mr. Marshall is the district attorney of Imperial County and they're right here in the law library," Della Street said, gesturing toward the open door.

"Well, I'll be glad to see them," Mason said. "Bring them in here, Della."

Mason was moving over to his desk as the two figures came from the law library, Baldwin Marshall in the lead, stalking determinedly, Latty hanging behind, as though just a little afraid.

Mason said, moving toward Marshall, "I presume you're

118

Baldwin Marshall—district attorney of Imperial County—right?"

"Right," Marshall said, extending his hand. "I believe you know Latty."

"Heavens, yes," Mason said. "I run into him every time I turn around. What is the reason for *this* visit?"

"You're representing Lorraine Elmore?"

Mason nodded.

"Montrose Dewitt was murdered in Calexico," Marshall said, "and we want to question Mrs. Elmore. We—"

"Murdered?" Mason interrupted.

"I think so," Marshall said. "Of course, I'll be frank with you, Mr. Mason. We're working largely on circumstantial evidence at the moment but there are some things about the case that I'm free to confess I can't understand. Mrs. Elmore seems to have played a rather peculiar part. . . . In fact, there seems to be a distinct conflict between some of her statements and the facts as we understand them."

"To whom did she make the statements?" Mason asked.

"To you," Marshall said.

Mason raised his eyebrows.

Marshall said, "I've heard a lot about you, Mr. Mason. You're supposed to be a dangerous antagonist who will rip me to pieces. You've had the background of years of experience and you're a genius in the art of forensic strategy.

"I'm a cow county district attorney. It may be I'm no match for you, but I'll tell you one thing, I'm not going to be afraid of you and I'm not going to be bluffed."

"That's most commendable," Mason said. "Now perhaps you can tell me what this is all about."

"Mr. Latty here," Marshall went on, "has some things on his conscience."

Mason regarded Latty curiously. "And came to you?"

"No," Marshall said, "I went to him. Latty tried to conceal what he knew for a while, but I sensed he was holding something back and . . . well, frankly, I put a little pressure on him, just as I'm going to put a little pressure on you."

"On me?" Mason asked.

119

"Exactly," Marshall said. "I have told you that I don't have your experience, I don't have your metropolitan background. Now I'm going to tell you something else; I have the law on my side. What's more, I have a majority of the voters in Imperial County back of me. If it comes right down to a fight, you can win the argument but by God you'll lose the case, because I'll throw the book at you just as quick as I would at anyone. Your reputation isn't frightening me a damned bit."

"I wouldn't want it to," Mason said. And then turning to Latty, said, "Just what is it that you were holding back, George?"

"Now, just a minute," Marshall said, "*I'm* going to do the talking here. You'll probably be cross-examining Latty on the witness stand, so I'm going to tell you some of the things I know, and then I'm going to tell you some of the things I want, and Latty is going to keep quiet."

Marshall turned to Latty. "You understand that?"

Latty nodded.

Marshall said, "Mrs. Elmore told you quite a story about having driven her car out on a side road. Someone forced Montrose Dewitt out of the car, marched him down the road a few feet, then clubbed him to death; then came back and told Mrs. Elmore to drive her car on ahead until she was stuck in the sand."

"She told me this?" Mason asked.

"Yes."

"And may I ask the source of your information?"

"You can ask," Marshall said, smiling, "and you won't get any answer. I'm asking you for a verification. Did she tell you this? Yes or no?"

Mason said, "Sit down. Make yourselves comfortable. Evidently this is going to be more than just a brief interview and—"

"It's all right, I don't mind standing," Marshall said, "and it's not going to be a long interview as far as I'm concerned. I want to know whether she made that statement to you."

Mason said gravely, "I am representing Mrs. Elmore. She's my client."

"So I understand."

"Therefore," Mason went on, "any statement she might have made to me is completely confidential. I couldn't repeat it."

"You certainly can tell me whether Mrs. Elmore was the victim of a holdup and an assault," Marshall said.

"I'm afraid I can't even tell you that," Mason said.

"Why not?"

"So far anything and everything I know about the case is information derived from sources I consider confidential."

"Now then, I'm going further than that," Marshall said. "You were in Calexico this morning. You had a chartered airplane. You got the pilot to fly low over some roads out to the west of Calexico until you located an automobile that was stalled in the sand. Then you had the pilot go back to the airport."

"And may I ask the source of that information?" Mason asked.

"I'm not going to be the one who answers *all* the questions," Marshall said.

Mason smiled. "I thought perhaps you would want to establish a precedent."

"I will, in this instance," Marshall said, "because I checked at the airport, found out the number of the plane you had, contacted the pilot and interviewed him."

"You seem to have been rather active," Mason said.

"I try to run down leads while they're hot," Marshall told him.

"A very commendable trait," Mason said. "I think you're going to prove a most dangerous antagonist."

"Do we have to be antagonists?" Marshall asked.

"That's up to you," Mason said. "Unless you charge my client with some crime, there's certainly no reason for us to assume adversary positions."

"I don't want to charge her with any crime unless she's guilty."

"Most commendable."

"But unless I can get some satisfactory answers to some of my questions, I will at least have to hold her as a material witness."

Mason smiled and said affably, "That will give her an opportunity to put up bond and I'm quite certain she has sufficient resources to put up any reasonable bond which a court may require."

"In that event I might have to go further and hold her for investigation."

"In which event," Mason said, "I would have to file *habeas corpus* and force you to either charge her or turn her loose."

"In which event, we'd charge her," Marshall said shortly.

"In that event, we would of course occupy the position of adversaries," Mason said, smiling.

"All right, I'll go further," Marshall said. "I have reason to believe that after you located that stalled automobile from the air, you left the plane at the airport, hurriedly took off in an automobile and drove out to the place where that car was parked. That car had a Massachusetts license plate and was the property of Lorraine Elmore, your client.

"You looked around at the scene, and I have reason to believe you took some evidence that you didn't want the authorities to find, and you may have left other evidence—or perhaps I'll put it this way, you may have left other objects which you *hoped* the authorities would consider evidence."

"Wouldn't that be unethical?" Mason asked.

"I think so."

"Yet you think I did it?"

"I'll put it this way: There's evidence indicating that you may have done so."

Mason was silent.

"Did you?" Marshall pressed.

Mason said, "No."

"You mean you didn't go out to that car?" Marshall asked. "You mean you didn't get out and look it over?"

"I didn't say that," Mason said.

"You said no."

"And I meant no. You asked me if I'd looked the car over, if I'd left objects which I hoped would be taken as evidence, if I had withdrawn other objects and I told you no."

"All right," Marshall said, "I'll split my questions up. Did you go out to the place where that car was stuck in the sand?"

"No comment," Mason said.

"Did you take anything out of that car?"

"No comment."

"Did you put anything in it?"

"No comment."

"All right," Marshall said, "that's all I wanted to know. I just wanted to know if you'd co-operate. You won't. Now then, I'm going to tell you something, Mr. Mason. I was prepared to give you every consideration. I was prepared to give your client every consideration. You have refused to co-operate with me so I'm under no obligation to co-operate with you.

"Up here in Los Angeles you seem to have the courts pretty well under the spell of your reputation. That reputation seems to dazzle the authorities. Down in my county, you're just another Los Angeles lawyer butting into a community where he's a stranger. I can throw the book at you and if I have to, I will."

"Go ahead and throw," Mason said. "I used to be good at catching and dodging. I'd dislike very much to lose my agility."

"I'll see that you have plenty of practice," Marshall promised, turning on his heel. "Come on, George."

"Wait a minute," Mason said. "Did you really expect me to answer all those questions, Marshall?"

"I asked them in my official capacity."

"That's not my question. Did you expect me to answer them?"

"No."

"Then why come up here to ask them?"

"Off the record," Marshall said, "I wanted to have the press in Imperial County tell the citizens of Imperial County that I had asked you those questions and that you had refused to answer."

"Like that, eh?" Mason asked.

"Like that," Marshall said, and escorted Latty out of the office.

Della Street looked at Mason with apprehensive eyes.

"Get Crowder," Mason said.

Della Street put through the call, then nodded to Mason when she had him on the line.

Mason picked up the telephone, said, "Duncan, this is Perry Mason. I've just had an official visit from your district attorney. There's been a leak."

"What sort of a leak?"

"A big one. Now, I want to know where it came from."

"Can you tell me more about it?"

"Any chance of your phone being tapped?" Mason asked.

"Hell, yes," Crowder said. "There's a good chance my phone is tapped and there's a good chance your phone is. The authorities pay lip service to the laws about wire tapping, but from what my friends who are skilled in electronics tell me, there are thousands of wire taps in existence. You and I could be among them."

"All right," Mason said, "I'll start asking questions. Has Dr. Kettle talked to anyone?"

"About what?"

"About anything his patient might have told him."

"I'll answer that one right off the bat," Crowder said. "The answer is no. Kettle, you can trust. He wouldn't talk to anyone."

"How about you? Have you talked to anyone?"

"Hell, no."

"I mean, even in confidence."

"No, I tell you."

Mason said, "This morning I had a Unit Nine there at the

124

Motel. Della Street had Seven. Howland Brent had Eleven, which adjoined me on the other side.

"I understand the walls are thin in that motel. I want to find out how thin. Go back there and rent Units Nine and Eleven and see what you can find out about voices carrying through the walls."

"Okay," Crowder said, "when do you want that done?"

"Now. I want to know if Brent could have heard everything we said in there."

"And when do I report?"

"Just as soon as you have the information. I'll wait here at the office."

"Okay," Crowder said, "I should be able to move in right away. Those units won't have been rented—unless, of course, Brent held onto his unit."

"If he did, get Units Seven and Nine and make a test," Mason told him.

"I don't think you have the same conditions," Crowder said. "Seven and Nine are in separate buildings. On the other hand, Nine and Eleven are in one building and there's just a door between them—a thin door. In case of necessity, that can be opened into a double cabin. The units are all designed that way, units of two in one building."

"Oh-oh," Mason said, "now I'm beginning to get the picture. Go take a look and give me a ring, will you, Duncan?"

"I'll take a look," Duncan said. "I'll take someone with me and we'll see how voices register. Do you want me to take a tape recorder and make a formal test?"

"No," Mason said, "this isn't for evidence. This is just for my own information."

"Okay, stick around. I'll call you back," Crowder said.

Mason hung up.

Della Street said, "What can he do?"

"Crowder?"

"Marshall."

"He can talk," Mason said. "He's talked. He can threaten. He's threatened. He can have our client arrested or he can

125

serve a subpoena on her to appear before the Grand Jury. He said a mouthful when he said he has the law back of him. He can do anything the law will let him do, and he can make a stab at doing some of the things the law won't let him do. . . . Now, what the hell do you suppose Latty told him that started all this? What do you suppose Latty has on *his* conscience?"

"Heaven knows," Della Street said.

"Well," Mason said, "Drake will have an operative pick up his trail and shadow him from the time he leaves here. We may find out a little more about him.

"You'd better put some coffee in that percolator, Della, and we'll kill a little time while we're waiting for Duncan Crowder to report."

"I have an idea it won't be long," Della Street said.

Mason grinned, nodded.

Della Street made coffee, brought out a package of cream-filled cookies.

Mason settled down with a sigh, munching on cookies, sipping coffee.

"This," he announced, "has been a fine, large day."

"And it was a fine, large night last night," Della Street said. "We got darned little sleep."

Mason nodded, yawned. "That's the way things go in the law business."

He finished his coffee, put the cup and saucer on the edge of his desk, settled back in the chair, closed his eyes and was almost instantly asleep.

Della let him sleep until Crowder's call came through from Calexico. Then she roused him. "Duncan Crowder on the line, Chief."

Mason picked up the telephone on his desk and motioned to Della Street to listen on her extension.

"Okay, Duncan," Mason said, "what did you find out?"

"I found out lots of things," Crowder said. "That place has been condemned down there. They either have to repair and change the construction or tear the place down. They're fighting it. Some of the units are more modern but some of

126

those units where they can make either a double or two singles out of one unit have walls that are like paper.

"Between Nine and Eleven there's just one thin door. By putting your ear up to the door you can hear ordinary conversation in the adjoining unit, if things are quiet. You can hear plain enough to get most of the words."

"I guess that's it," Mason said. "What about between Twelve and Fourteen?"

"The same situation exists there," Crowder told him. "Of course I didn't try Twelve and Fourteen, but I did take a look at the construction and know that it's another one of those units that can be rented either double or single, and I assume the same situation applies there."

"Okay, Duncan," Mason said, "we're in a fight down there. As soon as you can get to Dr. Kettle, relay a message to Lorraine Elmore. Tell her that she is not to answer any questions. She's not to make any statement to anyone under any circumstances."

"How soon do you want her to get that message?" Crowder asked.

"Before your district attorney can get back to his office," Mason said, "and preferably before he can telephone the sheriff."

"Will do," Crowder said cheerfully, and hung up.

# Chapter 12

At nine o'clock the next morning, Perry Mason used his latchkey to open the door of his private office, grinned at Della Street and said, "The dawn of a new day."

"I'll say," she said.

"What's new, Della?"

"Duncan Crowder called about five minutes ago. He wants you to call back."

"All right, get him on the line," Mason said. "What have we heard from Paul Drake?"

"Paul wants to make a personal report. He's had a lot of men working and has some information that he says is puzzling."

"Anything else?"

"Linda Calhoun called. She wants to know where her boy friend is."

"Where's she?"

"Calexico."

"The plot thickens," Mason said. "Let's try Crowder."

A few moments later when he had Crowder on the line, Mason said, "This is Perry Mason, Duncan. What's new down at your end?"

"Quite a bit," Crowder said. "My esteemed contemporary, Baldwin L. Marshall, seems to be out to make a record for himself."

"How come?"

"He's making quite an issue of local boy going up against the big-city slicker—kind of a David and Goliath thing."

"Where's he doing all this?"

"In the newspapers."

128

"Quotes?"

"Not direct quotes, but reports of the activities of our fearless prosecutor and statements from the quote, authorities, unquote. The *Sentinel*, down here, has been pretty much in his corner during the campaign and now they're really going to town."

"That's a local paper?"

"El Centro, the county seat."

"What's the line of attack?"

"The Imperial Valley David going up against the Los Angeles Goliath, making something of a partisan issue out of it. By the time we try to impanel a jury we'll find that it's the home team against the big, bad city slickers, and of course the jury, residing in the community, will be just a little partisan."

"Interesting," Mason said. "I guess this man, Marshall, is dangerous."

"He's dangerous; also he's ambitious."

"What else?" Mason asked.

"Well, it seems the main suspect at the moment is Lorraine Elmore. Marshall doesn't exactly say that Lorraine Elmore is a dope fiend but he has admitted to reporters that she was addicted to a very powerful sleeping medicine; that when she left Boston she managed to get her doctor to give her a prescription that should have lasted her for more than three months.

"For your information, the authorities are trying to trace this medicine. Apparently Lorraine Elmore took seven capsules during the interval between leaving Boston and arriving at Calexico. She took one capsule the night of the murder. One capsule was found on the front seat of the automobile. Approximately ninety capsules are not accounted for.

"The liquor which was found in the whiskey flask in the suitcase of Montrose Dewitt was simply saturated with this hypnotic.

"The authorities believe that Lorraine Elmore, who is under the care of a physician in a local hospital with no visitors permitted, was whisked away at the suggestion of none other than Perry Mason. Baldwin Marshall, our fighting district attorney, is said to have in his possession evidence indicating that as soon as astute defense counsel learned that the story told by Lorraine Elmore was in direct contradiction to the physical facts in the case, steps were taken to prevent the authorities from interrogating her."

"Well, that's interesting," Mason said. "It looks as though the case is going to be tried in the newspapers."

"Oh, perish the thought!" Crowder said. "Marshall deplores all this newspaper publicity. He says, however, that he feels the people are entitled to know what is being done in connection with the investigation of a mysterious death which begins to look more and more like deliberate murder."

"The newspaper doesn't say anything about any large sum of money Lorraine Elmore was supposed to have had?"

"No. The newspaper states that Marshall has announced to his intimate friends that he has had enough of being given the run-around; that these tactics may work in the large metropolitan areas but they are not going to work in a law-abiding, rural community; that at ten o'clock this morning he is going to call on Mrs. Elmore for a statement. If her private physician still insists that she is unable to give a statement at that time, he is going to ask the court to appoint a physician to examine her, and he intends to serve a forthwith subpoena on her, ordering her to appear before the Grand Jury."

"You've passed the word on to Mrs. Elmore that she isn't to talk?"

"I've told her not to give them so much as the time of day."

"Can we count on her?"

"I don't know, but I've impressed upon Linda Calhoun that she isn't to talk no matter what the circumstances. Linda Calhoun is a mighty sensible girl, Perry. She has her feet on the ground and her head on her shoulders."

"All right," Mason said. "Don't let Dr. Kettle get his neck stuck out too far. We're going to have to shift our position. Mrs. Elmore is not going to make any statement now on the advice of counsel."

"That means Marshall will take her into custody and charge her with murder."

"He's going to do it anyway," Mason said. "Now, here's one thing I want you to do, Crowder. If we're going to try this case in the newspapers, we'll do a little something ourselves."

"Okay, what do you want?"

"Ring up that doctor in Boston," Mason said. "Have an interview with him. You can point the direction of that interview. When you get done, you can make a statement to the press as the *local* attorney.

"Now, I want to accomplish several things by that statement. I want to let the people know that there's a local attorney, that it isn't simply the rural David against the big-city Goliath; that you are to take an important part in the case."

"I figured you'd want that," Crowder said. "What else? What do I do with the Boston doctor?"

"You point out to the doctor that Mrs. Elmore is at a period in life when romance is not dead; that she has been living in a small community under the watchful eyes of a neighborhood which is inclined to pity her as a relatively young and attractive widow; that there are no eligible men in the community; no social life; that, as a result, she has suffered from frustration and we understand he deemed it advisable to quiet her nerves with tranquilizers during the daytime and sedatives at night.

"When she left on the trip she was inclined to worry that she couldn't replenish her supply of sedatives, and he gave her a big supply, knowing that she did not have suicidal tendencies and knowing that her temperament was such that if she started worrying about not having sedatives when she needed them it would completely upset her nervous system.

"The large quantity of sedatives he supplied was simply

a psychological factor in connection with her treatment. He is familiar with her character and reputation. She is a woman of the highest integrity and there was no risk at all in prescribing a large quantity of sleeping capsules."

"You think he'll say that?" Crowder asked.

"Sure, he'll say it," Mason said. "He damned well has to say it. Otherwise he'd be put on the pan for giving a patient a prescription for such a large amount of powerful hypnotics. You can point out to him that *his* reputation is going to be put on the line and that before the press smears him, you think that it would be a good idea for the press to learn the true facts."

"And then tell him what the true facts are?" Crowder asked.

"Sure," Mason said. "Can you think of any more logical explanation?"

"I wouldn't even try," Crowder said modestly.

Mason laughed. "All right, Duncan, go to it. If they want to try the case in the newspapers, we'll give the newspapers a little something on which to base publicity that will favor the defendant, a poor, bewildered, frustrated widow, whose life was just opening up into a new vista of hope and promise when it was ruthlessly shattered again by the cruel hand of death. No wonder she's prostrated. The wonder is that she's retaining any vestige of sanity."

"I get it," Crowder said. "You want it spread on thick."

"Thick," Mason said.

"Okay," Crowder said, "can do," and hung up.

Mason grinned at Della Street. "If the D.A. wants to play rough, we'll play rough," he said. "That newspaper publicity is something two can play at."

"Well," Della Street said, "we seem to have the fat in the fire."

"We have a whole fire full of fat," Mason said. "Let's see what Paul Drake has to say for himself."

Della Street gave Paul Drake a ring, and within less than a minute the detective's code knock sounded on the door to Mason's private office.

Mason nodded to Della Street, who opened the door and let Paul in.

"Hi, Beautiful," Paul said. "What gives with you folks this lovely morning?"

"Gives, is right," Mason said. "We're having it thrust upon us."

"The D.A.'s tough?" Drake asked.

"He's— Well, let's say he's brash," Mason said. "He's playing the angle of local patriotism. He represents Imperial County, I represent the city slickers. We're going to do battle in front of a jury of Imperial County farmers and businessmen."

"But you have local counsel down there."

"He's brushing local counsel under the rug," Mason said. "The battle is between the bright, conscientious young D.A., filled with rural virtue, and the sophisticated city slicker who will resort to every trick in the book. Moreover, our client is a dope fiend, who is to be pitied, but that can't condone murder."

"How interesting," Drake said.

"The hell of it is," Mason said, "that I don't see how they can make a case out against Lorraine Elmore. When she tells her story, it is one thing; but she hasn't told her story."

"But they know what it is?"

"They seem to know what it is," Mason said, "thanks to the thin walls at the Palm Court Motel in Calexico. But I still don't get what they're trying to do. The case doesn't add up.

"The district attorney should be adopting a cautious attitude of saying, 'It's too early yet for us to tell exactly what happened but we want to question Lorraine Elmore, and the fact that she has an attorney who apparently wishes to keep her from being questioned is a suspicious circumstance.'

"If he'd adopt that gambit he'd put some pressure on me and would build up suspense as to what Mrs. Elmore's story was. Instead of that, he's apparently acting on the assumption he has a case against her and is laying the foundation for a favorable jury by feeding out information to the newspapers."

"Well, you can't blame him for that," Drake said. "He wants to win his case."

Mason's eyes glittered. "And I want to win mine, Paul. . . . But what about the various and sundry people you've been shadowing. Anything on them?"

Drake said, "Hold your hat, Perry. You're going to have a surprise."

"What?"

"Well, let's put it this way: two surprises."

"Start dishing them out, Paul."

"We'll start with Howland Brent. Now, there's a nice, conservative tweed-suited, pie-plate-hatted Boston investment counselor who suddenly goes hog-wild in Las Vegas, Nevada."

"Las Vegas!" Mason exclaimed.

"That's right. He drove a rented car to Palm Springs, then took a plane to Las Vegas, and really went to town."

"What do you mean, went to town? You mean he plunged?"

"Plunged all over the lot," Drake said, "and apparently made a killing."

"The hell he did!"

"That's right."

Mason said, "You never can tell about these conservative Easterners, Paul. They all of them have a streak in them of wanting to be Wild West. I'll bet if someone would give that fellow a twin-holstered rapid-draw gun belt with a couple of guns in it, he'd stand up in front of a mirror, practice a fast draw and take fiendish delight in the process. How much did he win?"

"You can't tell," Drake said, "but he did a peculiar thing. He got hotter than a firecracker. He had chips going all over the board in a big-time roulette game. People just gathered around to watch him. Boy, did he plunge!"

"And then what happened?"

"As nearly as we can tell the guy won about thirty-five thousand bucks."

Mason whistled.

"He certainly was a plunger. And then, all of a sudden something happened and he got cold as a cucumber."

"You mean he started to lose?"

"He started to lose," Drake said, "and he quit cold. He just walked away from the table and from then on he turned his back on every gambling device in Las Vegas. He wouldn't even put a nickel in a slot machine."

"Where is he now?"

"According to last information, he's sleeping late in Las Vegas. I have a couple of men tailing him and they're giving him a round-the-clock treatment. As soon as he gets up and gets in circulation, they'll phone the office."

"Good work, Paul," Mason said. "What's the other surprise?"

"Your friend, George Keswick Latty."

"What about him?"

"He's the fair-haired boy child of the district attorney of Imperial County," Drake said.

"How come?"

"After the district attorney left your office he seemed to have an idea that you might try to have them followed. He used routine precautions to throw a shadow off the trail, stuff that he's probably read about in magazines featuring detective stories, stuff that would have been effective ten years ago; but we were using an electronic shadowing device."

"How come?"

"A cinch," Drake said. "We checked the parking lot, found three cars that had licenses from Imperial Valley, looked at the registration certificates, found the one that was registered to Baldwin Marshall, put an electronic bug on it and had two men waiting in cars."

"And what did Marshall do?"

"Oh, he made figure-eights around the blocks, he went through traffic signals just as they were changing, he kept looking behind him, and finally became very smug and self-satisfied and then took Latty to—guess where?"

"Las Vegas?" Mason asked.

Drake shook his head. "Tijuana. In a chartered plane."

"Tijuana!" Mason exclaimed.

"That's right. Over the Mexican line. Any subpoenas you may try to serve on him will be valueless even if you find him. The guy is out of the jurisdiction of our courts and is in another country."

"Well, I'll be darned," Mason said.

"He puts this boy up at the best hotel in Tijuana," Drake said, "and explains to the clerk that the County of Imperial will pay for his room and board."

"And then?"

"Then Baldwin Marshall, feeling very much pleased with himself, flies back here in the chartered plane, picks up his car at the airport, drives to El Centro and starts dishing out interviews to his closest friends, who promptly relay the information to the public press."

"How interesting," Mason said.

"Now then, I have more news for you," Drake said. "Your friend has been subsidized."

"What do you mean?"

"I mean that the district attorney not only agreed to pay his room and board, but gave him a slug of money."

"You're sure?"

"The guy was broke, and now he's buying things," Drake said. "He has the attitude of the rich American tourist. He was probably instructed to act the part, and it's a part that suits George Latty to the ground. The guy's reveling in it."

Mason's eyes narrowed. "Paul," he said, "I don't care how many men it takes, put them on Latty's trail. Every time he buys something, find out how much it was. In other words, I want to find out every nickel that fellow spends.

"Then when the D.A. puts him on the stand, I'll teach Baldwin Marshall something about the practice of law that he may have forgotten. It's one thing to put a witness up in

136

a hotel where he won't be disturbed. It's quite another thing to hand a witness a bunch of cash for so-called expenses, particularly when the witness, who has been completely flat broke, goes out and becomes a heavy spender. In one case it's defraying expenses. In the other it's bribery.

"I wonder if George has let Linda know where he is."

"My best guess is that he hasn't," Drake said. "From the elaborate precautions that were taken by Marshall, I have an idea that Latty is completely incommunicado."

The telephone rang.

Della Street picked up the instrument, said to Mason, "Duncan Crowder calling from Calexico."

Mason nodded. "Stay on the line, Della," he said, and picked up his own instrument. "Hello, Duncan," he said.

Crowder said, "Got some news for you, Perry. What do you know about an ice pick?"

"An ice pick?" Mason asked.

"That's right. A murder weapon."

"Murder? I thought the guy died from an overdose of barbiturates."

"That's what everybody thought up to a short time ago," Crowder said, "but it seems the D.A. has been holding an ace up his sleeve. Evidently Dewitt was put to sleep with a dose of drugged whiskey, then somebody took an ice pick and stuck it in his head right above the hairline and then, with fiendish deliberation and wanting to make sure he was dead, stabbed him a couple of times in the heart.

"However, there wasn't any hemorrhage from the heart stabs, indicating that the man was already dead at the time those stabs were administered. The wounds on the body were so small that they could have been overlooked if it hadn't been for the fact that Marshall wanted a complete autopsy. He wired Los Angeles and had one of the best forensic pathologists come down to assist in the autopsy."

"Well," Mason said, "that changes the complexion of the case quite a bit."

"I'll tell you some more about the complexion of the

case," Crowder said. "They found the murder weapon in Lorraine Elmore's car."

"What!" Mason exclaimed.

"That's right, hidden under the floor covering in the baggage compartment, and moreover, the ice pick has been identified as one that came from Unit Sixteen of the Palm Court Motel—that's the unit that Lorraine Elmore occupied."

"How can they make that identification of an ice pick?" Mason asked.

"The units each have a bottle opener and an ice pick," Crowder said. "The numbers are stamped in the wood, small numbers that you wouldn't see unless you happened to be looking for them, but the landlady wanted to be sure that each ice pick was in its proper unit and so she numbered them—no particular reason except she had a numbering outfit and decided to stamp the numbers on the wood. She did the same thing on the bottle openers."

"So that's what's been in the background," Mason said.

"That's what's in the background, and Marshall is yelling for an immediate hearing. He wants Lorraine Elmore in court. Now, I can probably get Dr. Kettle to insist that there should be a sufficient delay to—"

"Hold everything," Mason interrupted. "Don't try for any delay. Let Marshall go right ahead.

"I want you to be rather inept and give the impression of being sort of dazed at the whole business. Let Marshall sweep along in a grand triumphant march and get the case into a preliminary hearing just as soon as he wants."

"The defendant is entitled to a continuance," Crowder said.

"I know," Mason said, "but you're not exactly certain of your rights. You sort of flounder around. It's going to put you in a bad light down there but I'll make it up to you later on."

"You've got a plan?" Crowder asked.

"Hell, no," Mason said, "I haven't got a plan, but I've

138

caught Baldwin Marshall sucking eggs. I've caught him bribing a witness."

"Bribing a witness!" Crowder exclaimed.

"It'll be that before I get done with it," Mason said, his eyes glinting. "You just let Marshall go ahead and set a date. The only thing is that you have to get in touch with me to find out just what my calendar is, and that will cause a little stalling around.

"I don't want the preliminary to take place until at least twenty-four hours have elapsed, but I don't want to go in and ask for a continuance on the ground of defense witnesses or constitutional rights."

"You want to let him try to deprive her of her constitutional rights?" Crowder asked. "That won't work if she's represented in court by counsel, will it?"

"She'll be represented in court by counsel, all right," Mason said, "and we're not going to rely on technical defenses about her constitutional rights, but I just want our friend, Baldwin Marshall, to give all the newspaper interviews and all of the tub-thumping possible and then I'm going to lower the boom on him by proving he's bribed a witness."

"That would be something," Crowder said.

"In fact," Mason said, "I think I'll let *you* bring out that evidence. That should give you a nice fat part in the play and keep the contest more on a local level."

"You interest me a lot," Crowder said. "By the way, Linda Calhoun is worried sick about Latty. What did you do to him?"

"I didn't do anything to him," Mason said.

"She thinks you did. She thinks you beat his ears back, put him on a bus and sent him back to Boston."

"I did nothing of the sort," Mason said.

"Well, where is he?"

"Hasn't he communicated with Linda?"

"No."

"That's funny," Mason said.

"It sure is," Crowder said, "because he should have been putting the bite on her."

"He certainly should have," Mason said. "The guy was broke and Linda wired him twenty dollars at El Centro. I gave him twenty dollars at Yuma, and he had gasoline to buy and then he had to pay for his room at the motel. Well, we'll probably be hearing from him pretty quick."

Mason turned to Drake and closed his eye in a wink.

"Okay. Anything else?" Crowder asked.

"That's it," Mason said. "We're starting for El Centro within an hour. Hold the fort until we get there."

# Chapter 13

Linda Calhoun and Duncan Crowder met Mason, Della Street and Paul Drake at the airport as the plane landed.

"Welcome back to Imperial County," Crowder said. "I've been dodging reporters. Knowing that the preliminary hearing is coming up tomorrow, they rather anticipated that you'd be here today and they want interviews."

"Why not?" Mason said.

"You mean you're willing to be interviewed?"

"Certainly."

"I didn't know. I thought I'd put it up to you first. This man, Marshall, is full of tricks. Some of them are rather clever."

"So I understand," Mason said.

Linda Calhoun said, "Mr. Mason, I want you to find out what's happened to George Latty."

"Something has happened to him?" Mason asked.

"I don't know. I think so."

"You haven't heard from him?"

"I've heard from him. Just a brief message, but I don't know where he is now."

"What was the message?" Mason asked.

"He called up the hotel when I was out and asked if he could leave a message. The operator told him that he could. He said to tell me that circumstances which he couldn't explain at the present time necessitated that he keep out of the picture for a while; that he was all right, that I wasn't to worry, but that he couldn't communicate with me, and that he was going to have to trust to my loyalty."

"I see," Mason said.

"Do you suppose he's all right?" she asked.

"That," Mason said, "depends on what you mean by all right. Do you mean, is he sober, is he leading a moral, upright life, is he loyal to you, or do you mean is he safe?"

"At the moment I mean is he safe?"

Mason said, "I would gather from the message that he is safe."

"But where in the world is he?"

Mason said, "I can't tell you that, Linda, and I want to point out once more that I'm representing your aunt. I'm doing it at your request, but she's my client. Her interests come first."

"But what does that have to do with George?"

"I can't even tell you that," Mason said. "It may have a lot, it may not have anything to do with him, but there are some things on which I can't afford to take any chances."

She said, "I have a peculiar feeling that you and Duncan are keeping things from me, Mr. Mason."

Mason glanced at the young attorney as he heard Linda Calhoun use his first name so easily and naturally.

Crowder, interpreting his glance, grinned and said, "Linda and I are on a first-name basis, Perry."

"So I see," Mason said.

Linda flushed slightly, turned to Paul Drake. "You're investigating the facts in this case, Mr. Drake. Don't *you* have any idea where George is, or what has happened?"

Drake grinned. "A detective gets lots of ideas, Miss Calhoun, but many times they don't pay off."

Della Street took Linda's arm. "I'm satisfied there's nothing to worry about, Linda," she said.

"But I can't understand it. George is— Well, he doesn't have a great deal of initiative in financial affairs and he has no money. He came out here to be with me and— Well, it's simply that this is not like him, that's all."

Mason said, "I think the police have probably interrogated him as to what he knows."

"And just what *does* he know, Mr. Mason?"

"That," Mason said, "is hard to tell. He was of course there in the motel and he said that the walls were paper-thin.

142

An inspection of the unit he was occupying shows that it was one side of a double unit and the other side was occupied by Montrose Dewitt. Under those circumstances he might very well have heard something."

"No doubt he did," she said, "but why didn't he tell me, and what does that have to do with his disappearance?"

"I can't tell you," Mason said.

"Do you know?"

Mason said, "Let's put it this way, Miss Calhoun. We'll go to Duncan's office. You can call up the district attorney and ask him point-blank if he knows anything about George or any reason why George shouldn't communicate with you."

"Would he tell me?"

"Is there any reason why he shouldn't tell you?"

"Not that I know of."

"Well, let's go do that," Mason said, giving Crowder a quick glance. "You can talk on one phone, and Duncan and I will listen in on extensions and we'll see if the district attorney knows anything about this."

"Once you get to my office," Crowder said, "you're going to have a problem with newspaper reporters."

"We'll cross that bridge when we come to it," Mason said. "Right now I'd like to hear what Marshall has to say in response to Linda Calhoun's question."

They drove to Crowder's office, where Linda put through the call to Baldwin Marshall, the district attorney.

Perry Mason and Duncan Calhoun listened in on extensions.

"This is Linda Calhoun, Mr. Marshall," Linda said, as soon as she had the district attorney on the line.

"Oh, yes, Miss Calhoun," Marshall said, his voice combining a synthetic cordiality with cold caution.

"I'm trying to find out what has happened to George Latty," she said. "I thought perhaps you could help me."

"What makes you think anything has happened to him?"

"I haven't heard from him."

"Not at all?"

"Just one brief, cryptic message telling me not to worry about him, that he'd have to trust to my loyalty."

"But he told you not to worry."

"Yes."

"Are you worrying?"

"Yes."

"He must have sent you that message for *some* reason," Marshall said.

"I'm quite certain he did."

"And he went to some trouble to tell you that you weren't to worry."

"Yes."

"And here you are, worrying."

"But I want to know where he is."

"I'm afraid I can't help you there."

"Well, let me ask you a direct question. Do you know where he is?"

There was a moment's hesitation, then Marshall said, "No, Miss Calhoun, I'll be frank with you. I don't know where he is."

"But you think that he's all right?" Linda persisted.

"I think if he told you not to worry that I wouldn't worry. I'd have that much confidence in him, and in the integrity of his friendship, regardless of what any other persons might say.

"Now, let me ask you a question, Miss Calhoun. Did you make this call of your own volition?"

"Why, yes, certainly."

"I mean, did anyone suggest to you that you should call me and ask that question?"

She hesitated.

"Did your attorney, Perry Mason, suggest that you should call me and ask me where Latty is?"

"Why ... I ... I was worried and—"

"Yes, thank you very much," Marshall said. "I was quite satisfied Perry Mason was behind your inquiry, and let me ask you another question. Is Perry Mason perhaps listening on the line?"

Linda Calhoun gasped.

"Right here," Mason said. "Good morning, Marshall."

"I thought perhaps you had inspired this call," Marshall said. "If I have any inquiries of you, Mason, I'll ask them man to man and not try to hide behind the skirts of some woman."

"I'm not hiding behind the skirts of some woman," Mason said. "I'm simply checking on your statements. I don't want her to talk with you unless I hear what's being said."

"Well, you know what's been said now," Marshall said.

"I heard you very distinctly," Mason said. "I heard you state that you don't know where Latty is."

"I've told Miss Calhoun, and I'm telling you, that I don't know where George Latty is," Marshall said, and slammed up the telephone.

"Now I *am* worried," Linda said.

"I'm sorry I can't help you," Mason said. "You're going to have to adjust yourself to the situation."

"But what's the situation?"

"That," Mason said, "remains to be determined. I'm satisfied that Latty is not in any physical danger—at least I feel quite certain he isn't."

Crowder's secretary said, "Two reporters are in the office insisting that they have an opportunity to interview Mr. Mason."

"Let them come on in," Mason said.

Crowder nodded and the secretary opened the door.

Two reporters and a newspaper photographer entered the office. One of the reporters said, "Mr. Mason, I'm going to ask you a question straight from the shoulder. Were you talking with Baldwin Marshall on the phone just now?"

Mason said, "I was talking with Baldwin Marshall on the phone."

"May I ask the reason for the conversation?"

"Miss Calhoun is somewhat concerned about the absence of her fiancé, George Latty. She thought that perhaps Marshall might know where he was. She rang him up and asked him, and I listened in on the line."

"Then you weren't talking with Marshall, you were simply listening."

"I was talking with Marshall."

"Would you mind giving me the gist of your conversation?"

Mason hesitated.

"Were you offering to plead Lorraine Elmore guilty of manslaughter if he'd reduce the charge?"

"Heavens, no," Mason said. "What gave you that idea?"

"There's a rumor to that effect."

"Inspired, perhaps, by the district attorney?" Mason asked.

"I don't know where it came from. All I know is that there's a rumor. We've heard it and lots of people have heard it."

"For your information," Mason said, his eyes suddenly hard, "there was nothing of that sort in the conversation and there is nothing of that sort in our minds—absolutely no intention of making any such absurd offer.

"I can also tell you that I did talk personally with Marshall after Miss Calhoun had finished her conversation. I can further state that Marshall assured Miss Calhoun and assured me that he did not know the whereabouts of George Latty."

"Why's Latty so important?" the reporter asked.

"That is something I'm not prepared to discuss at the moment," Mason said.

"Why not?"

"I don't have the necessary information."

"Let me ask you this. The preliminary hearing is scheduled to start tomorrow at ten o'clock. Are you going to ask for a continuance?"

"It's always difficult to look into the future," Mason said, smiling. "But, as you can see, Mr. Crowder is here; I'm here, and thanks to the efforts of Baldwin Marshall and the sheriff, Lorraine Elmore, the defendant, is going to be available."

"Does that mean you're going to be ready to proceed with the preliminary?"

"It could," Mason said. "However, I'd like very much to talk with George Latty before we went ahead."

"Why? Is he a witness?"

"Not for us."

"Is he for the prosecution?"

"I can't tell about the prosecution."

One of the reporters said, "Look, you're certain that Baldwin Marshall told you he didn't know where Latty is?"

"That's right."

"But why should Latty disappear?"

"I'm sure I couldn't say."

The other reporter said, "The word is being passed around that you're either going to offer to plead guilty to a lesser crime tomorrow, or that you won't put up any defense and will consent to having the defendant bound over for trial."

"Where do those rumors originate?" Mason asked.

"Well," the reporter said, "one of them originated right in the office of Baldwin Marshall. He stated positively and absolutely that he was not going to accept any offer to let Lorraine Elmore plead guilty to manslaughter and take that plea."

"Did he say any overtures had been made along those lines?"

"He said that he was not going to consider the proposition."

"Ask him," Mason said, his eyes glinting, "if anyone has made him any such a proposition, and if he says that anyone representing the defendant has, you can state that Mr. Mason would, under those circumstances, call him a liar."

The reporters started scribbling gleefully.

"If," Mason went on, "the district attorney has conveyed any impression that anybody connected with the defense has offered to plead Lorraine Elmore guilty to manslaughter in order to secure a dismissal of the murder charge thereby, Mr. Marshall has stated facts that were not so."

"Well, wait a minute," one of the reporters said, "actually all he said was that he would not consider the proposition. He didn't say that one had been made."

"All right," Mason said, "under those circumstances you can state that we will not consider any proposition which may be made by the D.A. for Mrs. Elmore to plead guilty to simple assault. We want a complete vindication."

The reporter broke out laughing. "May I quote you on that?"

"You may quote both of us," Mason said. "Don't forget that Duncan Crowder is in this case."

"We won't forget," the reporter assured him, "and we'll be covering the case tomorrow."

Mason grinned. "So will we," he said.

The reporters left the office.

When the reporters had left, Drake made a significant gesture to Perry Mason, and Mason followed him into a private office.

"That district attorney is lying," Drake said.

"About Latty?"

"About Latty. Latty is staying across the line in Mexicali right now. He's registered at a hotel under the name of George L. Carson. He called the district attorney's office not over an hour ago and had a long talk with Marshall."

"What else is he doing?" Mason asked.

"He's living it up," Drake said. "He got just a little plastered last night. He had a dinner of roast venison, tortillas, frijoles and champagne. He had a side dish of two quail but he bogged down before he finished and only ate one of the quail. He finished the champagne, however, and was feeling no pain as he wended his way back to the hotel. He's planning on being available tomorrow at the preliminary hearing, but he isn't coming over until the district attorney sends for him. He's going to be a surprise witness and he evidently has some evidence that Marshall feels is going to be a bombshell for the defense."

Mason said, "Marshall is quite a chap, isn't he, Paul?"

"Are you going to call him a liar in court?"

Mason raised his eyes. "What did he lie about?"

"Why, he said right out, didn't he, that he had no idea where Latty was?"

"He assured Linda that he couldn't tell her where Latty was—that he didn't know."

"Well?" Drake asked.

Mason said, "Linda wasn't smart enough to ask him if he knew where Latty had been half an hour ago, or an hour ago, or at any time during the morning. She simply asked him if he knew where Latty was, and he said he didn't. His exact words were, 'No, Miss Calhoun, I'll be frank with you. I don't know where he is.'"

"Why didn't you nail him on that?" Drake said. "If he's taking advantage of that kind of a technicality, why didn't you come right out and ask him if he knew where Latty had been earlier in the day?"

Mason said, "If I'd done that, I'd have let him off the hook."

"What do you mean, off the hook?"

"He's hooked," Mason said, smiling. "He's been so smart he's outwitted himself."

"How come?"

"I'm going to bring the matter up in open court tomorrow. I'm going to assure the court that we had the solemn statement of the district attorney that he didn't know anything about where Latty was. That will bring the district attorney to his feet, stating that he told us no such thing, that he said he didn't know where Latty was at the moment we were telephoning; that Linda had asked him, 'Do you know where George Latty *is*?'"

"Well?" Drake asked.

"And, by the time he gets done," Mason said, "or by the time I get done with him, he's going to look like a shyster, a crook and a liar. Whereas, if I had asked him if he knew where Latty had been earlier in the day, he'd have told me to go to hell and hung up and if I'd tried to take the matter up in open court, then *I* would have been the one that wasn't reporting the entire conversation.

"Tomorrow I'm going to be dignified, injured and perhaps just a little dazed by the rapidity of developments. We'll let Marshall do the explaining."

"Are you going to be an injured martyr or are you going to get mad?" Drake asked.

"It depends on which way will do my client the most good," Mason told him.

"My best hunch is you should get mad," Drake said.

"We'll think it over," Mason said.

"Won't you get mad anyway?" Drake asked.

"A good lawyer can always get mad if somebody pays him for it, but after you've been paid a few times for getting good and mad, you hate like the deuce to get mad on your own when nobody's paying you for it."

Drake grinned. "You lawyers," he said.

"You detectives," Mason told him. "Keep your men on the tail of George Latty."

"We've got men looking down his shirt collar right now," Drake said.

# Chapter 14

Judge Horatio D. Manly took his place on the bench, regarded the packed courtroom, said, "This is the time heretofore fixed for the preliminary hearing in the case of the People of the State of California versus Lorraine Elmore."

"Ready for the People," Marshall said.

"Ready for the defense," Mason said, placing a reassuring hand on the shoulder of Lorraine Elmore.

Judge Manly cleared his throat. "Before this case starts, I want to state that there has been a lot of newspaper publicity about the case, about the facts, and about the people involved. I want to caution the spectators that this is not a show, this is not a debate, this is not entertainment. This is a court of justice. The spectators will comport themselves accordingly; otherwise the Court will take steps to insure proper decorum."

Mason stood up. "May I be heard?" he asked.

"Mr. Mason," Judge Manly said.

"It happens," Mason said, "that the defense is very anxious to get in touch with one George Latty. We have reason to believe that the prosecution is either keeping Mr. Latty concealed, or knows where Mr. Latty is, despite the fact the district attorney has given his verbal assurance that he does not know where Latty is."

"Just a minute, just a minute," Marshall said, getting to his feet, "I resent that."

"Are my facts incorrect?" Mason asked.

"Your facts are incorrect."

Mason said, "I was a party to a telephone conversation yesterday, Your Honor, at which time the district attorney assured Linda Calhoun, the niece of the defendant, that he did not have any idea where George Latty was. I would like to have that statement repeated in open court."

"Now, that's simply not so," Marshall said. "I did not make any such statement."

"You didn't?" Mason asked in surprise.

"I did not. Miss Calhoun asked me specifically, 'Do you know where Mr. Latty is?' and I told her I didn't know. I had no way of knowing. I was talking with her on the telephone. I didn't know what he was doing at the moment, or where he was at that particular moment."

"Oh, *at the moment!*" Mason said. "But you didn't *say* that to her. You said that you didn't have the faintest idea where he was, or words to that effect."

"I think that counsel is deliberately misquoting me, Your Honor," Marshall said.

"Well, so there may be no misunderstanding at the moment," Mason said, "do you know where Latty is now, or do you know where he was an hour ago, half an hour ago, or twenty-four hours ago; or can you tell me how Linda Calhoun can get in touch with Mr. Latty? Linda Calhoun and George Latty are engaged to be married, Your Honor."

"I don't have to answer your questions. I don't have to submit to your cross-examination," Marshall said. "I'm running the district attorney's office, not a matrimonial agency. If Latty wants to get in touch with Linda Calhoun, he certainly can do so."

"Unless he has been instructed not to," Mason said. "And, so there can be no misunderstanding, I will ask counsel if he did or did not instruct Latty not to get in touch with Linda Calhoun."

"I certainly did not do any such thing," Marshall said. "In fact, I specifically instructed Latty *to* get in touch with Linda Calhoun."

Mason raised his eyebrows. "And tell Miss Calhoun where he was?"

"I didn't say that," Marshall said.

"Well then, perhaps I should express myself differently,"

Mason said, "and ask you if you didn't instruct Mr. Latty specifically *not* to tell Linda Calhoun where he was."

"I don't have to answer your questions. I don't intend to be cross-examined by you," Marshall said.

"In short," Mason said, "I think the Court can see the technicalities, the equivocation, the dodging, the subterfuges, the evasions, which have characterized the prosecutor's office in connection with our attempts to locate George Latty. I wish the Court would instruct the district attorney to disclose Mr. Latty's present whereabouts to the defense."

Mason sat down.

"Do you know where Latty is?" Judge Manly asked Marshall.

"If the Court please, that isn't a fair question," Marshall said. "Let the defense attorney state that he wants to use Latty as a defense witness, and then there would be some reason for the inquiry. We don't have to disclose our knowledge to defense counsel simply to facilitate some budding romance between a relative of the defendant and an important witness for the prosecution."

Judge Manly glanced at Mason.

Mason rose with dignity and said, "If the Court please, we don't know whether Latty will be a witness for the defense or not. We haven't had an opportunity to question him since certain matters came to our attention. It might well be that we will desire to use him to establish some points in connection with the defense of this case."

"If the Court please," Marshall said, "they haven't the faintest intention of putting on any defense. This entire furor over the whereabouts of George Latty is simply for the purpose of embarrassing the prosecution."

"Well," Judge Manly said, "I'll get back to my question: Do you know where Latty is?"

"Certainly, we know where he is," Marshall said. "He's a witness for the prosecution and we're keeping him where he won't be tampered with."

"May I ask what the prosecution means by being tampered with?" Mason asked.

"Being influenced so that his testimony will be changed," Marshall said. "Because of his romantic entanglement with the niece of the defendant, this witness would be in a position where shrewd and unscrupulous counsel could get him to change his testimony."

Mason said, "Do you mean that this witness is so vacillating that he might change his recollection of what he knew or what he saw by being exposed to contact with a relative of the defendant?"

"You know what I mean!" Marshall shouted. "I mean that *you* could bring pressure to bear so that you'd have this young man all mixed up."

"If," Mason said, smiling, "the district attorney now admits that his appraisal of his own witness is that the witness can't stand interrogation by anyone other than the prosecution without changing his testimony, I'm quite willing to accept that statement."

"That isn't what I said! That isn't what I meant and you know it!" Marshall shouted, his face dark with anger.

Judge Manly said, "Gentlemen, gentlemen, that's enough. The remarks of counsel in the future will be addressed to the Court. Now, the Court will ask you, Mr. Prosecutor, since it now appears you know where George Latty is, is there any reason why his whereabouts can't be disclosed to the young woman to whom he is engaged, or why defense counsel can't serve a subpoena on him?"

Marshall said, "He's in the office of the district attorney, waiting to be called as a witness for the prosecution in this case—as a most important witness, I may say."

"Then," Mason said, "I take it, Your Honor, that Miss Calhoun can be assured that the failure of her fiancé to get in touch with her and disclose his whereabouts was due to the fact that the witness was acting under orders of the prosecution."

"Miss Calhoun isn't a party to this action. She doesn't have to be assured of anything," Marshall said.

Judge Manly said, "Do I understand that you expect to produce George Latty in this courtroom, Mr. Prosecutor?"

"He will be here within an hour," Marshall said.

"Very well," Judge Manly said, "I think that answers the question. Regardless of what has been done in connection with concealing or not concealing the whereabouts of this witness, or the reason for it, the witness will be present in court and counsel will have an opportunity to question the witness as to where he has been and why he failed to communicate with—"

"But I consider those questions would be entirely improper, Your Honor," Marshall interrupted. "Latty is only a witness. He's not a party to a controversy."

Mason said, "Counsel may *always* examine the bias of a witness, and any witness who is so completely biased, so completely under the control of the prosecution that he is willing to forego communicating with his fiancée in order to further the interests of the prosecution's case, can certainly not be considered a fair and impartial witness. The defense should have a right to inquire into his motivation."

"I would certainly think so," Judge Manly said.

Marshall said, "Your Honor, we would like to argue the point later on when the question comes up."

"Yes. There's no need for a discussion at this time," Judge Manly said. "I'll rule on the matter when the witness is called to the stand."

"I take it, the prosecution promises to call him," Mason said.

"The prosecution doesn't have to disclose its witnesses to the defense."

"You have already assured the Court that you would call Latty as a witness within the hour."

"I expect to call him," Marshall said.

Mason smiled and bowed graciously to the Court. "If the prosecution had only made that statement earlier, it would have saved a lot of time and perhaps some recriminations."

Marshall, thoroughly angry, said, "I don't like being forced to disclose my case to the defense in advance."

"Well, you've disclosed it now," Judge Manly said. "Call your first witness."

Marshall seemed ready, for the moment, to argue the matter with the Court but finally, and after frantic whispering on the part of his deputy who sat beside him at the counsel table, said, "I will call the county surveyor as my first witness."

The county surveyor introduced a diagram of the Calexico motel, a map of the roads out of Calexico, and located on the map the place where Lorraine Elmore's automobile had been found.

There was no cross-examination.

The sheriff, called as a witness, testified to finding the automobile stuck in the sand and to the presence of a capsule on the front seat.

"Do you know what that capsule contained?" Marshall asked.

"I do now, yes."

"And do you have that capsule with you?"

"I have."

"Will you produce it, please?"

The sheriff produced a small bottle from his pocket. Within that bottle was the green capsule.

"And what does this capsule contain?" Marshall asked.

Crowder glanced at Mason. "Want to object?" he whispered.

Mason shook his head.

"The capsule," the sheriff said, "contains Somniferal."

"And do you know what that is?"

"Yes, sir."

"What is it?"

"It is one of the newer forms of hypnotics. It is quite powerful and has the peculiar property of taking effect very quickly and lasting for a long time. For the most part, the hypnotics which take rather quick effect are soon dissipated, whereas the hypnotics that last for a long time are slower acting. This relatively new drug, Somniferal, which

156

is, by the way, a trade name, is both quick in its action and long lasting."

"Did the defendant tell you anything about this capsule?" Marshall asked.

"She refused to make any statement concerning it, saying she was doing so on the advice of counsel."

"Did you," Marshall asked, "ever find the container from which this capsule was taken?"

"Yes," the sheriff snapped. "In the defendant's handbag."

Crowder watched Mason anxiously, then seeing that the lawyer was making no move to object, leaned closer and whispered, "That's a conclusion. He *can't* know what container the capsule came from."

Mason smiled, placed his lips close to Crowder's ear. "Don't object to those things," he said. "That's the mark of an amateur. Let the evidence go in and then get the guy all flustered on cross-examination. Remember now, when you cross-examine him, bear down on the point of *how* he knew it was this container. Get him to show that he's relying on hearsay evidence. Ask him if he didn't know that was improper. Ask him if he didn't discuss this phase of his testimony with the district attorney—if the district attorney didn't tell him in effect, 'I'm going to ask you this question and you answer it fast before the defense can object. It's hearsay but we'll try and get it in anyway.' Show his bias."

"Wait a minute, wait a minute," Crowder whispered, "when *I* cross-examine him?"

"Sure, you," Mason said. "You want to get your hand in, in this case, don't you?"

"My gosh, I'd love it," Crowder said, "but I didn't know that you were going to let me take part in the examination of witnesses."

"Don't you want to?"

"Heavens, yes. I— There's a young lady in the courtroom that I'd— Well, frankly, I'd like to have an opportunity to impress her."

"You'll have the opportunity," Mason said.

Judge Manly, noticing the colloquy between counsel,

said, "The question asked the sheriff was whether he had ever discovered the container from which this capsule had been taken and he said that he had; that it came from a bottle which was found in the handbag of the defendant in the Calexico motel."

"Were those capsules dispensed on a prescription?" Marshall asked.

"They were."

"Did you talk with the physician who dispensed the prescription?"

"Yes."

"Where was he located?"

"In Boston, Massachusetts."

"He is not here as a witness?"

"No."

"But nevertheless he did explain to you why he had issued a prescription for an unusually large number of these capsules?"

"Yes."

"I have no further questions at this time. You may cross-examine," Marshall said, bowing to Mason as though by giving him an opportunity for cross-examination he was generously conferring upon defense counsel a very great privilege, all in the interests of fair play.

Mason jerked his head toward Crowder. "Go ahead, Duncan," he said.

Crowder said, "You have stated, Sheriff, that this capsule contained Somniferal?"

"That's right."

"And how do you know it contained Somniferal? Was it analyzed?"

"I had the prescription."

"What prescription?"

"The prescription under which the capsule was purchased."

"And where did you get the prescription?"

"From the doctor who issued it."

"Did you have the original prescription?"

"Certainly not. The drugstore has that."

"Oh, then you *didn't* have the prescription."

"Not the original."

"And you didn't have the capsule analyzed?"

"Certainly not. The capsule is intact."

"Then how do you know it is a capsule from this prescription?"

"Because the label is on the bottle."

"And the bottle was found where?"

"In the unit of the motel occupied by the defendant."

"And how do you know the capsule came from that bottle, Sheriff?"

"Because it's the same kind of a capsule that was in the bottle."

"How do you know it is?"

"Well, it has the same color, the same physical appearance."

"Then you know that the capsule came from the bottle, because the bottle was reported to have contained Somniferal, and you know the capsule contained Somniferal because you deduce it came from the bottle. Or, to put it the other way, because you assume the capsule contained Somniferal, then it must have come from the bottle which you assume contained Somniferal because someone told you over the long distance telephone line that it contained Somniferal."

"That's not a fair way of putting it," the sheriff said.

"All right," Crowder said, "put it in what you consider a fair way then."

"Well, I talked with the doctor who issued the prescription and he told me what was in the prescription. I checked . . ."

"Yes, yes," Crowder said, "keep right on, sheriff. You checked what?"

"Well, I checked the contents of the bottle with the prescription the doctor told me over the telephone he had issued to the defendant."

"Then you didn't go to the trouble of telephoning the

drugstore that had filled the prescription, giving them the number on the bottle and getting *their* version of the contents?"

"No. I didn't think that was necessary."

"Do you know generally that hearsay evidence is inadmissible?"

"Certainly."

"Didn't you realize all this was hearsay evidence?"

"Well, it was the only way we could get the evidence. We couldn't have these people come on from Boston, just to testify to something that was perfectly obvious."

"And how do you know this capsule came from the bottle?"

"Because it's the same size, shape and color."

"Is there anything about the size or shape that would differentiate it from any other three-grain capsule?"

"The color is distinctive."

"And the color is green?"

"Yes."

"And did the doctor tell you that Somniferal was put up in capsules and the color was green?"

"No, he didn't."

"Who did?"

The sheriff squirmed uncomfortably. "A druggist in El Centro."

"And is that druggist here to testify?"

"Not that I know of."

Crowder said, "If the Court please, I move to strike out all the testimony of the sheriff relating to the nature and contents of the capsule, and the contents of the prescription bottle, upon the ground that it now appears the entire evidence was based upon hearsay and conclusions."

"Oh, Your Honor," Marshall said, "here we go, with a lot of petty, technical objections dreamt up by my young erudite friend. By the time he's practiced law a little longer he'll learn that on the nonessentials we grant professional courtesies and a certain amount of give and take."

"We haven't seen any giving yet, Your Honor," Crowder

said. "It's all taking. No one knows what's in that capsule. The prosecution has assumed it's Somniferal because they have assumed it came from that bottle, and they have assumed the bottle contained Somniferal, because a doctor in Boston said it did, but there isn't any proof as yet that the capsule ever came from that bottle."

"Your motion is granted," Judge Manly said. "The testimony is stricken in regard to the drug in this capsule."

"But, Your Honor," Marshall said angrily, "this goes to the very gist of the case. We want to show that the deceased was given a drink of drugged whiskey; that the whiskey was drugged with Somniferal. We want to show that the defendant had that drug in her possession."

"Show it by competent evidence and we have no objection," Crowder said, "but we're not going to have the entire case against this defendant built upon a structure of hearsay testimony and pure assumptions on the part of the authorities."

"The Court has ruled on the matter," Judge Manly said.

"But, Your Honor, this is just a preliminary examination," Marshall protested.

"And the same rules of evidence apply as in any court of law," Crowder snapped.

"I think that is technically correct," Judge Manly said. Then added in a more kindly voice to the district attorney, "Perhaps you can connect it up later."

"Not without having a witness fly out here all the way from Boston," Marshall said.

"The defense will be only too glad to consent to a continuance so the witness can be brought out here," Crowder said affably. "We would like very much to cross-examine the doctor in question, to find out how he knows what was in the bottle and how he was able to identify the bottle on the telephone. I think it will appear that the doctor only issued a prescription and had nothing to do with filling it. Only the druggist could tell what's in the capsules."

"Well, we'll have the druggist fly out here too, if that's what you want," Marshall said.

Crowder smiled. "All *I* want is to have the prosecution introduce competent evidence and not rely on hearsay evidence."

"The Court has ruled," Judge Manly said. "You'd better call your next witness and try to connect it up later on, Mr. District Attorney."

"Very well," Marshall snapped with poor grace, conscious of the fact that the newspaper reporters were scribbling copious notes. "I'll call Hartwell Alvin, chief of police of Calexico."

"Very well," Judge Manly said. "Come forward and take the stand, Chief Alvin."

Alvin, a tall, cadaverous individual in his fifties with expressionless eyes which seemed to hide behind an opaque film, came forward, held up his hand, was sworn, and took his seat on the witness stand. His manner was calmly detached.

"Your name is Hartwell Alvin and you are now and have been for the last several years chief of police of Calexico in Imperial County, California?"

"That's right," Alvin said.

"Directing your attention to the morning of the fourth of this month, did you have occasion to go to the Palm Court Motel in Calexico at an early hour in the morning?"

"I did."

"Now, since counsel wants to object to all hearsay testimony, I won't ask you what it was that caused you to go there, because anything you learned over the telephone would be hearsay. But just tell us what you found at the time you arrived."

"I found a dead man in Unit Fourteen."

"Did you know this man?"

"No."

"Was he subsequently identified?"

"Yes."

"Was he identified as being a certain Montrose Dewitt of Los Angeles?"

"That's right."

"What time did you arrive at the unit?"

"Shortly after seven."

"In the morning?"

"That's right."

"What else did you find?"

"I found the body of this man lying on the floor of Unit Fourteen. I found that things were disturbed in the room as is shown in photographs which I had taken. That is, some of the drawers were open and a suitcase and bag were open. I found a state of much greater confusion in Unit Sixteen. Drawers had been pulled open, things spread out on the floor, baggage was open, and clothing and other objects had been strewn all over the floor."

"You took photographs of these units?"

"I did. That is, I caused them to be taken."

"And you have prints of these photographs?"

"I have."

"Will you hand them to me, please, and tell me as you hand them to me, what each one represents."

There was a period of some minutes during which the witness handed the prosecutor photograph after photograph, and explained what was shown in each photograph, the position from which it was taken, and in which unit it was.

"Did you consult the register of the motel?" Marshall asked.

"Yes. Unit Sixteen had been rented to a person using the name of Lorraine Elmore, and Unit Fourteen to a person registered under the name of Montrose Dewitt."

"Were you with the sheriff when an automobile, registered in the name of Lorraine Elmore, was found in the desert?"

"I was."

"Did you look around in the vicinity of that automobile?"

"I did."

"Did you take photographs?"

"That was later. I caused the photographs to be taken."

"Do you have those photographs with you?"

"I have prints, yes, sir."

Again, Alvin introduced half a dozen prints showing the car stuck in the sand.

"Did you find anything in the car?"

"I did."

"What?"

"In the baggage compartment underneath the floor covering I found an ice pick."

"Do you have that with you?"

"I do."

"Produce it, please."

The witness produced the ice pick, which Marshall asked to have marked for identification.

"I show you the figure sixteen on this ice pick and ask you if that figure was stamped in the handle of the ice pick when you found it?"

"It was."

"Did you find anything else?"

"I saw the sheriff pick up a greenish capsule on the front seat of the automobile."

"Were you present when the sheriff found a bottle with a prescription number?"

"I was."

"Where was that found?"

"In Unit Sixteen, in a small handbag."

"You may cross-examine," Marshall said.

Mason whispered to Duncan Crowder, "Take him on, Duncan. There's not very much you can do with him. Don't generalize. Pounce on one point that you can emphasize and then let him go."

Mason sat back and watched the young man with keen interest.

Duncan Crowder rose, smiled at the chief of police, said, "As I understand your testimony, and as I observe from these photographs, Unit Sixteen had been pretty much taken to pieces."

"That's right."

"Someone had disturbed the baggage, the contents of the drawers in the dresser."

"That's right."

"Did you look for fingerprints?"

"We tried to develop latents, yes."

"And did you develop any latents?"

"We did."

"Why didn't you mention those in your testimony when you were being examined by the prosecutor?"

"He didn't ask me."

"Why didn't he ask you?"

Marshall was on his feet. "Your Honor, I object to this as improper cross-examination and assign it as an improper question. This witness can't read the mind of the district attorney."

"Sustained," Judge Manly said.

Crowder smiled. "I'll reframe the question and put it this way. Did you discuss the case with the prosecutor?"

"Certainly."

"Before you went on the stand?"

"Yes, of course."

"And you went over with him what your testimony was going to be?"

"Yes."

"And did the prosecutor, at the time of that conference, state to you that he didn't want you to say anything about the latent fingerprints you had discovered unless you were specifically asked, and tell you that he wasn't going to ask you about the fingerprints on direct examination?"

"That's objected to, if the Court please," Marshall blurted angrily. "That conversation, or any conversation this witness may have had with the prosecutor, has no bearing whatever on the case. I am not on trial here."

Crowder said, "But if it should be made apparent that the witness deliberately shaped his testimony and deliberately withheld certain facts from his direct examination at the request of the prosecutor, that would show bias on the part of

165

the witness, Your Honor, and would be perfectly proper on cross-examination."

"I think that is correct," Judge Manly said. "The objection is overruled."

"Answer the question," Crowder said.

Marshall apparently debated whether to argue the point further. He stood for an uncertain moment or two, then reluctantly sat down.

The witness said, "He told me not to say anything about the fingerprints unless I was asked."

"Did he say why?"

"He said that it was simply going to confuse the issue."

"All right, *I'll* ask you about the fingerprints. What did you find?"

"There were fingerprints of Lorraine Elmore, the defendant. There were fingerprints of Montrose Dewitt."

"In both cabins?"

"In both cabins."

"Go on. What other latents?"

"There were fingerprints that had been made by the maid who makes up the rooms, and there were several latent fingerprints which couldn't be identified."

"They were sufficiently clear so an identification could be made?"

"If we can find the person whose hand made those fingerprints, the latents are clear enough so a match can be made."

"You have photographs of those latent fingerprints?"

"I have."

"Produce them, please."

"If the Court please," Marshall said, "the witness can be asked about what he found on cross-examination, but the defense has no right to introduce photographs of what was found as part of cross-examination. If the defense wants those fingerprints in evidence, they can call this witness as a defense witness and put them in."

"Oh, I think not," Judge Manly said. "This witness was asked what he found; he photographed the interior or had photographs taken and those were introduced in evidence. Now, if photographs were deliberately withheld at the request of the district attorney and that is brought out on cross-examination, counsel has a right to have those photographs of the fingerprints introduced."

"I object, if the Court please, to the statement that they were deliberately withheld on the advice of the district attorney."

"You may object to it," Judge Manly said, "but it's part of the evidence. I'm simply commenting on the evidence."

The witness produced the fingerprints, and Crowder had them introduced in evidence.

"Now then," Crowder said, pleasantly, "the indication in those units was that some person had very hurriedly searched the baggage and the drawers as though looking for something. Is that right?"

"That's right."

"But that same condition could have existed if a person had been planting some evidence such as this prescription bottle in the baggage somewhere. Isn't that right?"

"Well, not exactly. If a person had been planting something, it would have been planted in one place and all of the other baggage wouldn't have been disturbed."

"Well then, I'll put it this way," Crowder said. "If some person had searched the baggage in order to make sure that some object *wasn't* in the baggage and then, having found that the object was not in the baggage, had planted another similar object so that investigators would be sure to find it, the condition of things in the units would have been just about as you found them."

"That's right," the witness conceded. "When you find things disturbed that way, you can't tell whether anything was taken or whether a person was just looking for something, and unless you have an inventory of what was in the room in the first place, you can't tell what's missing and you can't tell what's been added."

"Thank you very much indeed for an impartial statement of the situation, Chief," Crowder said with a little bow. "I appreciate your frankness and we have no further questions."

"There's no need for defense counsel to make a speech," Marshall said.

"Oh, he was simply thanking the witness," Judge Manly observed, a twinkle in his eye.

"Well, he has no right to do that."

"Perhaps not," Judge Manly said, "but there's no jury present and it isn't going to hurt anything, and while we're on the subject the Court also wants to thank the witness for being commendably frank. You're excused, Chief Alvin."

Alvin left the stand.

"Call Ronley Andover," Marshall said.

Mason turned to raise a quizzical eyebrow at Paul Drake, who, in turn, shrugged his shoulders, indicating that he had had no previous knowledge that Andover was to be a witness.

Andover was sworn, took the stand, gave his name and address.

Marshall said, "Did you see a body at the office of the coroner? A body that was listed on the coroner's records as that of Montrose Dewitt?"

"I did."

"Did you know that individual in his lifetime?"

"I did."

"And what was the name under which you knew him?"

"That of Weston Hale."

"Did you share an apartment together?"

"We did."

"Do you know whether this individual had a relatively large amount of cash on his person when he left Los Angeles?"

"Yes, sir."

"How much was the amount?"

"Fifteen thousand dollars."

"You may cross-examine," Marshall snapped.

Mason nudged Crowder and said, "I'll take him, Duncan."

Mason got to his feet. "How do you know that he had fifteen thousand dollars, Mr. Andover?"

"Because I gave it to him."

"And where did you get it?"

"I cashed a check which Weston Hale made to me in an amount of fifteen thousand dollars and turned it over to him."

"Do you know whether Weston Hale was the man's right name or whether it was an alias?"

"I believe Weston Hale was the man's right name."

"Do you have any idea why he took the alias of Montrose Dewitt?"

"No."

"Did you know that he maintained an apartment under the name of Montrose Dewitt, and a separate entity and a separate bank account?"

"I know it now. I didn't know it then."

"You gave this money to Weston Hale?"

"I did."

"When?"

"On the third."

"Where?"

"He stopped at the apartment we shared."

"He came up to the apartment?"

"No, he asked me to come down and meet him on the sidewalk."

"You did?"

"Yes, sir."

"Was he driving his own car?"

"No, sir. He was riding as a passenger in a car which was being driven by the defendant."

"Did he get out of that car?"

"He did not. He simply drove by, and I handed him the envelope containing the money."

Mason frowned thoughtfully, then said slowly, "I have no further questions."

Marshall called the coroner and then the surgeon who had performed the autopsy, brought into evidence the existence of the wounds in the head and in the torso; wounds which had been made by a long, thin object "similar to an ice pick."

Then Marshall called the manager of the motel, brought out from her that each unit had been equipped with ice picks, that these ice picks were similar in appearance and design to the one that had been found in the automobile registered in the name of Lorraine Elmore, and that each ice pick had had stamped on its handle the number of the apartment in which it belonged, and that the number 16 on this ice pick would indicate that it had been taken from Unit 16.

Crowder looked to Mason for instructions.

Mason shook his head. "No cross-examination," he said. "You've done fine so far. Just let these witnesses go."

Baldwin Marshall arose and said dramatically, "If the Court please, my next witness will be George Keswick Latty, and at the conclusion of his testimony counsel for the defense can cross-examine him to their heart's desire."

"That remark is uncalled for," Judge Manly said. "If Latty is to be your next witness, call him and dispense with verbal flourishes."

"Yes, Your Honor," Marshall said, "but in view of the fact that there had been an intimation that I was afraid to let defense counsel interrogate this witness I simply want them to know he will be available for interrogation."

"Well, you don't need to let them know anything of the sort," Judge Manly said. "They have a right to cross-examine any witness you put on the stand, and," the judge added, his color deepening, "in view of your declaration that they can examine him to their heart's content, the Court is going to take you at your word and the cross-examination will be virtually unlimited as far as this Court is concerned. Now call your witness."

"Mr. Latty to the stand," Marshall said, apparently not in the least concerned with the Court's rebuke.

There was a moment's wait while all eyes turned expectantly to the doorway of the courtroom. Then Latty, escorted by a police officer, stood dramatically in the doorway, his chin in the air, his pose that of a man fully conscious of the dramatic possibilities of the situation. Then, his chin still elevated, he strode down the aisle to the witness stand, held up his right hand, was sworn and was seated on the witness stand.

His eyes caught sight of Linda and he smiled, the gracious smile which royalty bestows upon a loyal subject.

"Your name is George Keswick Latty," Marshall said, "and you are engaged to be married to Linda Calhoun, who in turn is the niece of the defendant. Is that right?"

"Yes, sir."

"Very well. Now, I will ask you where you reside."

"In Massachusetts. Near Boston."

"You are attending a university there?"

"Yes, sir."

"When did you leave there?"

"On the morning of the third."

"By plane?"

"Yes, sir. By jet plane."

"And where did you go?"

"To Los Angeles."

"Whom did you see in Los Angeles?"

"Linda Calhoun."

"That is the niece of Lorraine Elmore?"

"Yes."

"And did you discuss the affairs of Lorraine Elmore with Linda?"

"I did."

"Now, I'm not going to ask you for that conversation because that would be hearsay and not binding on the defendant, but I am going to ask you if as a result of that conversation you took any action?"

"I did."

"What?"

"We went to consult Perry Mason on the morning of the third."

"Now, again without disclosing conversations, I take it

that at the time you consulted Perry Mason the situation was, generally, that Linda and her aunt had quarreled over—"

"Just a moment, Your Honor," Mason interrupted. "I object to the question on the ground that it is obviously leading and suggestive and calling for hearsay evidence."

"Sustained," Judge Manly snapped.

"All right," Marshall said angrily, "if I can't prove it directly, Your Honor, I'll prove it by inference. What did you do after you left Mason's office, Mr. Latty?"

"I rented an automobile."

"And what did you do with that rented automobile? Where did you go?"

"I shadowed Lorraine Elmore in her automobile."

"And where did that shadowing lead you?"

"She was joined by Montrose Dewitt. Then she put a lot of baggage in an automobile and they started south, after first stopping at the curb to receive an envelope from a man I now know was Ronley Andover."

"What did *you* do?"

"I followed them until I lost them about ten miles or so before we came to Arizona."

"And what did you do after that?"

"I continued on into Arizona."

"Did you see anyone there whom you knew?"

"Yes. I saw Perry Mason and Paul Drake, the detective."

"And then what happened?"

"Then I returned to El Centro. I telephoned Linda from El Centro, and she told me that she had heard from the defendant, Lorraine Elmore, and that Lorraine was staying at the Palm Court Motel in Calexico."

"So what did you do then?"

"I had intended to return to Los Angeles, but since the motel in Calexico was only some ten or twelve miles from El Centro, I decided to drive down and look the situation over."

"And you did so?"

"Yes."

"What time did you arrive in Calexico?"

"I don't know the exact time. It was shortly before midnight."

"And what did you do?"

"I drove to the Palm Court Motel. I checked on the cars in the parking place and found that Lorraine Elmore's car, with its Massachusetts license plates, was parked there in the motel."

"What did you do?"

"I noticed that the car was parked in front of Unit Fourteen. I also noticed there was a vacancy sign so I registered and was given a unit nearer the street. I asked if there wasn't something farther back and was offered Unit Twelve, which I accepted."

"Now, where was Unit Twelve with reference to the unit occupied by Montrose Dewitt?"

"Montrose Dewitt was in Unit Fourteen and I was on the west adjoining his unit."

"What did you do after you checked into your unit?"

"I explored the situation."

"What do you mean by that?"

"Well, I looked the place over."

"What did you find?"

"Apparently Unit Twelve and Fourteen were so designed that they could be rented as one double unit in case the parties renting the units wished to open them up into one double unit. I found that there was a door which was locked, but someone had bored a small hole in this door—a hole made with a very small drill, but it enabled one to see into the adjoining unit."

"Could you hear through this door?"

"Not very well through that door. I could see through it and could see a very small section of the room on the other side. However, by going into the clothes closet and putting my ear against the wall of the clothes closet, I could hear conversation in the adjoining unit quite plainly."

"What did you do?"

"I looked through the small hole which had been drilled

in the connecting doorway. I could see a portion of the bed in the adjoining unit. I saw Montrose Dewitt and Lorraine Elmore sitting side by side on the bed. I could see they were talking but I couldn't hear what they were saying, so I left that door and went into the closet. By going to the extreme end of the closet and putting my ear against the partition, I could hear what was being said."

"All of the conversation?"

"Not all of it, but nearly all of it."

"Now then, just what did you hear?" Marshall asked.

"There was some discussion of a personal nature."

"What do you mean by that?"

"Well, they were . . . well, what we call pitching a little woo."

"You mean they were making love?"

"Well, not exactly love. They were doing a little necking and making a little . . . verbal love."

"All right," Marshall said, turning to smile at the crowded courtroom, "now let's go on from there. Did you hear them discussing their future plans?"

"I did."

"What did they say?"

"Mr. Dewitt told Lorraine that Linda was simply trying to get her money, that she wanted to dominate Lorraine and force Lorraine to live the kind of a life Linda wanted for her, a life of seclusion, a life of austerity, one that was barren of affection; that it was the sort of life that would lead to premature age and that Linda didn't have Lorraine's interests at heart."

"Then what?" Marshall asked.

"Then Lorraine became indignant and told him that he had misjudged Linda, that Linda was impulsive but that when she once had a chance to get acquainted with him they would both like each other; Lorraine said she felt very repentant about having quarreled with Linda and that she had called Linda up and asked her forgiveness and told Linda that she would see her the next afternoon; she added

174

that she and Dewitt would be married by that time and that she wanted Dewitt to meet Linda."

"All right," Marshall said, "just go on from there. What happened after that?"

"Well, then Dewitt became very much enraged when he heard that she had telephoned Linda. He said, 'I told you not to communicate with her. I told you that we were going to have to live our own lives, that we'd make this joint investment without letting anyone know we had done so and would cash in for a couple of million dollars within twelve months.' Then, he said, Lorraine could let her friends know where she was and what she was doing. She'd be a rich woman by that time."

"Go right ahead," Marshall said. "What happened after that?"

"Well, Lorraine was angry and hurt. She said that she was reasonably well fixed right now; that she didn't have to sacrifice her friendship with her family in order to make more money; that money wasn't everything in life."

"And then what?" Marshall asked.

"Well, then he apologized for losing his temper and started using terms of endearment and she didn't respond very well. She said that she didn't see any reason why she should sever all connections with her family just because they were starting out again in life, and they talked for a while and then she said good night, that she was going over to her cabin."

"And did she?" Marshall asked.

"She started for her cabin and got as far as the door and then Dewitt saw something in the parking place which alarmed him. He said something about a car. By that time they had moved away from the bed and were standing in the doorway and I couldn't hear very well, but he said something about a car and then there was a lot of motion and not much talk, and suddenly the lights went out and I heard Lorraine's car start.

"I dashed to the door and looked out into the parking

area and saw the two of them in Lorraine's Massachusetts car, just pulling out of a parking space."

"Who was driving?" Marshall asked.

"She was."

"Who do you mean by she?"

"Lorraine."

"And whenever you have used the word Lorraine, whom do you mean?"

"Lorraine Elmore, the defendant in the case, the person sitting there beside, and a little behind, Perry Mason."

"So what did you do?" Marshall asked.

"I tried to follow them. I ran and jumped in my own car, started the motor. By the time I got to the street they had reached the corner and had made a turn. I knew I didn't have time to make any wrong guesses. I felt that they had turned to the left toward town, so I skidded into a left-hand turn and then found that I'd make a mistake. They weren't ahead of me. I was going to make a U-turn but saw a police car parked up the block so I had to make a run around the block, and by the time I got back to the intersection I'd lost all track of them. I cruised around for about an hour trying to find them and couldn't."

"Then what did you do?"

"Then I took the road out of town and followed it as far as the junction with the Holtville road."

"And then?"

"I couldn't find them so I returned."

"Go on," Marshall said.

"Well, I was very much chagrined. I felt I had made a complete failure of everything. I knew that Mr. Mason would make some more of his sarcastic remarks and I was afraid of the effect he and his remarks would have on Linda. So I felt pretty low. I waited around for fifteen or twenty minutes, I guess, and then decided that they'd skipped out and the only thing to do was to get some sleep, so I went to bed and I was tired. I was asleep almost instantly."

"What wakened you?"

"The sound of voices in the adjoining motel unit."

"By the adjoining motel unit now, you are referring to Unit Fourteen, the one that Montrose Dewitt occupied?"

"Yes."

"And what happened?"

"Well, I jumped out of bed and hurried to the place in the closet where I could listen."

"You didn't try to look?"

"No, I could look through the door but I could hear through the closet and because someone was talking I wanted to hear what it was."

"And what did you hear?"

"I heard Dewitt's voice saying how sleepy he was; that he had never been so tired in all of his life, and then he said something to the effect that 'We're in the big-time now. We've got it made,' or something of that sort, and then he started talking, mumbling, his voice sounding as if he might be talking in his sleep. I could hardly understand him.

"Then he started to say something about suitcases and I heard him pick up a suitcase and put it down on the floor and then I heard a heavy thud."

"What do you mean by a heavy thud?"

"Like the sound made by somebody falling to the floor, collapsing."

"And then what happened?"

"I was trying to account for that sound. At first I thought it might have been a suitcase. Then, while I was still thinking, I heard someone moving around and I thought that was Dewitt."

"Never mind what you thought," Marshall said. "You heard the sound of a thud and then you heard someone moving around."

"That's right."

"And what did you do?"

"I continued to listen, hoping that there would be more conversation."

"There was none?"

"No."

"So then what did you do?"

"So then I left the closet and went to the door, hoping I could see what was going on, because with someone moving around I felt certain that that person would sooner or later come within my line of vision."

"Did that happen?"

"No. Just as I got there the lights went off and everything was dark and silent in the cabin."

"So then what?"

"I stood there thinking the matter over and finally remembered what Dewitt had said about being tired and decided he had gone to bed, and that Lorraine had gone back to her own—"

"Never mind what you decided," Marshall said. "That's not proper for you to state. Just state what you said, what you heard, what you saw, what you did."

"Well, I went back to bed and lay there for ten or fifteen minutes but couldn't sleep and finally decided I would take a look and see if there was a light in Lorraine's cabin. So I got up and started to dress."

"You say you *started* to dress."

"That's right."

"What happened?"

"I heard a door slam in the adjoining unit; in Fourteen."

"You heard it *slam*?"

"That's right."

"And then what?"

"I ran to the door just in time to see the taillight of an automobile turning from the parking space into the highway."

"Could you recognize the automobile?"

"Not to be absolutely certain about it. I couldn't see the license number."

"Well, what car did you *think* it was?"

"Objected to as calling for a conclusion of the witness," Crowder said.

"Sustained," Judge Manly said. "The witness said he

couldn't recognize the car. What he thought is of no importance in this case."

"Well, what did you *do*?" Marshall asked.

"I finished dressing just as fast as I could, again jumped in the car and went out and made a search. This time I didn't make such a long search. I swung around town but couldn't find any trace of Lorraine's automobile, so I went back to my unit, went to bed and tried to sleep but couldn't make it. Along about five or five-thirty in the morning I got up and dressed, took my car, and went to a restaurant and had breakfast. When I returned Perry Mason was there at the motel, and very shortly afterwards I went in and started to shave. It was about that time I heard a scream. I wasn't certain just where the scream had come from but I got to thinking things over and finally decided I'd better investigate. I went to the door of my cabin, standing there partially shaved, in my undershirt and trousers and then learned of the murder."

Marshall turned to Mason with a bow. "Now go ahead and cross-examine," he said, "and I can assure you there will be no objections from the prosecution. Just ask any questions you want."

Judge Manly rapped on the desk with the tip of a pencil. "Mr. Prosecutor," he said, "the Court is not going to warn you again. I don't want any side remarks from counsel and there is no reason for you to make it appear that you are granting the defense a concession in connection with the cross-examination of a witness."

"I *was* making a concession, if the Court please," Marshall said. "I was stating that I would make no objection to any questions they wanted to ask on cross-examination."

"Proceed with the cross-examination," Judge Manly said.

Mason rose to look searchingly at the witness.

For a moment Larry met Mason's eyes defiantly. Then he shifted his gaze and also shifted his position in the witness's chair.

"So you're engaged to Linda Calhoun?"

"That's right."

"How long have you been engaged?"

"Something over five months."

"Has a wedding date been set?"

"We're waiting until I finish law school."

"Who is furnishing the funds to put you through law school?"

Marshall jumped to his feet. "Oh, if the Court please," he said. "This is—"

"Sit down," Judge Manly snapped. "You said you weren't going to object to any questions defense counsel might ask. You said it several times under such circumstances that the Court feels it constitutes a stipulation. Any objection you want to make is overruled. Now, sit down."

"But this is so manifestly improper," Marshall said.

"It may show bias," Mason said.

"I don't care what it shows," Judge Manly snapped. "The understanding was you could cross-examine this witness to your heart's content and there would be no objection. As far as this Court is concerned, you can go right ahead."

"My fiancée is advancing the money that will enable me to complete my education and then I will repay it."

"You'll repay it by marrying her?"

"I expect to, yes."

"And then the monies that you earn will be community property."

"I haven't given that matter any thought."

"Now, when was the last time you saw Linda Calhoun before you came to court a short time ago?"

"I saw her on the third."

"That was the last time you saw her until you walked into court today?"

"I— Well, I— That was the last time I spoke to her, yes."

Mason, watching the witness's manner, said, "I'm asking you when was the last time you *saw* her?"

"Well, I *saw* her very briefly on the street at Mexicali."

"When?"

"Yesterday."

"Did you speak to her?"

"No."

"How close were you to her?"

"She was about half a block away."

"Did you make any effort to catch up with her?"

"No."

"What did you do?"

"I went to my hotel and telephoned the hotel where she was staying."

"Did you ask for her on the phone?"

"Yes."

"That was immediately after you had seen her on the street in Mexicali?"

"Yes."

"Then you knew she wouldn't be in her hotel."

"Yes."

"And what happened? What did you say over the phone?"

"I asked for Linda and when I was told that her room didn't answer I asked if I could leave a message for her and was advised that I could, so I left her a brief message telling her not to worry about me, that I was all right."

"So you put through that call when you knew she wouldn't be in her room?"

"She couldn't have been two places at the same time."

"But you waited until you were certain that she was out of her room before you called."

"Not necessarily."

"You sent her that message because you thought she would be worrying about you?"

"Naturally."

"It had then been some time that she hadn't heard from you?"

"Yes."

"A day or two?"

"Yes."

"And you sent that message telling her not to worry because you loved her and because you knew that she would be worried about you and wondering where you were."

"Yes."

"Then why didn't you send that message earlier?"

"Because . . . because I was told that no one was to know where I was staying."

"Who told you that?"

"The prosecutor, Mr. Baldwin L. Marshall."

"And you obeyed his commands?"

"I prefer to state that I complied with his requests."

"To the extent of letting your fiancée worry about you?"

"I just told you that I sent a message so that she wouldn't worry about me."

"But you didn't send that until you were assured that she wasn't there so she could receive your call."

"Well . . . yes."

"So you did nothing to alleviate her worries for some twenty-four hours."

"That's right. I've admitted that."

"Just because the district attorney told you not to."

"He said it was important that no one should know where I was. I asked him if I could let my fiancée know, and he said I could leave a message for her but he didn't want me talking with her. He didn't want anyone to see me."

"Now, you went directly from your conference with the district attorney to Mexicali?"

"No, I went first to Tijuana."

"To Tijuana!" Mason exclaimed in apparent surprise. "And how long were you in Tijuana?"

"Overnight."

"And then you went to Mexicali?"

"Yes."

"By bus?"

"No."

"By private car?"

"By chartered plane."

"Who took you over there?"

"Mr. Marshall, the district attorney."

"And did Mr. Marshall mention my name during the ride?"

"Oh, Your Honor," Marshall said, "this is going so far afield that it is ridiculous! What I talked about with this witness is completely outside of the issues. It has no bearing on the case. The conversation is not admissible. There has been nothing in the direct examination of this witness to warrant asking such a question and I object to it."

"The objection is overruled," Judge Manly snapped. "You go right ahead, Mr. Mason. You ask any questions you want to that would tend to show bias on the part of this witness."

"If the Court please," Marshall said, "anything of that sort doesn't show bias. It simply shows that I was taking reasonable precautions to see that the defense didn't know all about my case."

"We won't argue the matter," Judge Manly said. "A ruling has been made." He turned to the witness. "The question was: Did Mr. Marshall mention Mr. Perry Mason's name?"

"Yes."

"More than once?" Mason asked.

"He discussed you at some length."

"He mentioned my name more than once?"

"Yes."

"More than twice?"

"Yes."

"More than three times?"

"Yes."

"More than ten times?"

"I didn't count them."

"But it could have been more than ten times?"

"It could have been."

"And you mentioned my name?"

"Yes."

"And the district attorney told you, did he not, that he wanted particularly to have your story hit the defense in this case as a bombshell and that he was going to take every precaution to see that you didn't tell the story to anyone?"

"I believe so, yes."

"And the district attorney went over and over your story with you?"

"Yes. We talked about what I had seen quite a bit. He kept asking me to think back and see if I couldn't amplify my testimony a little."

"Oh, the district attorney wanted you to *amplify* your testimony, did he?"

"Well, he— Not exactly that."

"You just said that he asked you if you couldn't amplify it a little bit."

"Well, the word amplify was my interpretation of what he said."

"All right," Mason said, "as nearly as you can remember what the district attorney said to you, the effect of it was that he wanted you to amplify your evidence, is that right?"

"Yes."

"And he gave you money to do so?"

Marshall was on his feet. "Your Honor, this is a matter of personal privilege. I object to this. This is not proper cross-examination. This is a dastardly insinuation! It is a lie!"

"You object to the question?"

"Yes, I do."

"The objection is overruled. Sit down."

"Answer the question," Mason said. "Did Marshall give you money?"

"Not to amplify my testimony."

"Did Marshall give you money?"

"Yes."

"You were entirely dependent on Linda Calhoun for your spending money?"

"Well, I had a little savings account."

"A *savings* account!"

"That's right."

184

"Saved from what?"

"From my allowance."

"What allowance?"

"What Linda gave me. I told you all about that."

"And did Linda know you had put aside this little nest egg?"

"No."

"Linda was working?"

"Yes."

"And depriving herself of the little luxuries of life, the things that mean so much to a young woman, in order to give you money so you could put yourself through law school?"

"Yes."

"And you were embezzling some of that money?"

"What do you mean, I was embezzling it?" the witness shouted. "It was given to me."

"It was given to you for a specific purpose, was it not?"

"I suppose so."

"And you took some of that money and held out on your sweetheart. You deposited it in a savings account so you could use it for some other purpose."

"Not for another purpose, no."

"It was given to you to defray your living expenses while you were going through law school?"

"Yes."

"And you didn't use it for that purpose?"

"I had more than I actually needed."

"You didn't send the surplus back?"

"I did not. I made a lot of economies myself, Mr. Mason. I went without things that I wanted in order to help out."

"In order to help who out?"

"Linda."

"Then you should have sent the surplus money back to Linda if you were economizing to help her."

"I told you I put the surplus in a savings account."

"In your name?"

"Yes."

"Now, you saw me on the evening of the third in Yuma, Arizona?"

"Yes."

"And told me you were broke?"

"Yes."

"And I gave you twenty dollars?"

"Yes."

"Then you immediately went back to El Centro and telephoned Linda and told her you were broke and asked her to wire you twenty dollars, did you not?"

"I asked her for funds so I could get home, yes."

"And told her to wire you twenty dollars and waive identification?"

"Yes."

"You told her you were broke?"

"Yes."

"But at that time you had twenty dollars I had given you, did you not?"

"Well, that was a loan."

"You intended to repay it?"

"Certainly."

"But you had it?"

"Yes."

"And you knew that I gave it to you to defray expenses?"

"No, you didn't give it to me for any such purpose."

"I didn't?" Mason asked.

"No, sir. You did not. You told me to take that money and go to a motel in Yuma."

"So you took the money and then didn't go to the motel?"

"I changed my mind."

"But you had the money."

"I considered that money was in trust for a certain specific purpose, Mr. Mason. You had told me to go to a motel in Yuma. I decided not to do so. Therefore I didn't want to use your money. I telephoned Linda and asked her to wire me money."

186

"So then what *did* you do with the twenty dollars I had given you?" Mason asked. "Did you mail it to my office address, stating that you were sorry you—"

"No, of course not. I had it with me."

"And how long did you keep it?"

"I ... I can repay you now."

"I'm not asking you to repay me *now*. I'm asking you how long you kept it."

"Well, I still have it."

"You didn't spend it?"

The witness hesitated, then said, "No."

Mason said, "You were in Tijuana. You were staying at the best hotel there."

"Yes."

"Your expenses were paid?"

"I paid my expenses."

"From the money Linda had sent you?"

"No, that was all gone."

"What money did you use?"

"Money Mr. Marshall had given me."

"You looked around and saw the sights in Tijuana?"

"Yes."

"Did you bet on race horses?"

The witness hesitated, then said, "Yes."

"More than once?"

"Yes."

"Now, did the district attorney give you money to bet on the horse races?"

"He didn't say what I was to do with it."

"He just handed you a sum of money?"

"Yes."

"How much?"

"A hundred and fifty dollars the first time."

"The *first* time!"

"Yes."

"There was, then, a second time?"

"Yes."

"How much was given you at that time?"

"A hundred and fifty dollars."

"So you have received three hundred dollars from the district attorney?"

"Yes."

"Any more?"

"Well ... he okayed my expenses at the hotel in Mexicali. He told the hotelkeeper to give me anything I wanted and to charge it to the county here. He said the county would honor a bill from the hotel."

"So you charged things in the hotel?"

"Yes."

"And used the money I had given you to bet on the horse races?"

"I did no such thing."

"You used the money the district attorney had given you to bet on the horse races?"

"Well ... yes."

"And the district attorney gave you money for the purpose of betting on the horse races?"

"Certainly not."

"Then why did you use the money for that purpose?"

"It was my money. I could do what I wanted to with it."

"The money wasn't given you for expenses?"

"I ... I assume so."

"What was said when the money was given to you?"

"He didn't say anything. He just handed me the money and told me that I'd be needing some money."

"You paid your expenses out of this money?"

"Well ... yes."

"And then started betting on the horses."

"I ... I had to do something. I was shut off from all of my friends. I was forbidden to get in contact with anybody."

"All right," Mason said, "now let's get back to the times the district attorney mentioned my name. What did he say about me?"

"Objected to," Marshall said. "Not proper cross-examination, no part of the issues."

188

"Overruled," Judge Manly snapped.

"He said you were a big-time lawyer and that he didn't want to have to be afraid of you and that he'd— Well, that he was going to get you down here in his county where the newspapers were friendly and give you a shellacking."

"And he wanted you to help him do it?"

"He said my testimony was going to be of great help."

"And he wanted to keep me from finding out what that testimony was going to be?"

"Well, he said he didn't want me to talk with anyone."

Mason said, "Now, you went to a curio store while you were in Mexicali, did you not?"

"Yes."

"And you bought some curios?"

"Some souvenirs."

"For your friends?"

"Yes."

"And for yourself?"

"Yes."

"And you bought a rather expensive camera, did you not?"

"Well . . . yes."

"What became of the camera?"

"I have it with me."

"Where?"

"In my suitcase."

"Did you tell the district attorney you had bought this camera?"

"No."

"What did you pay for the camera?"

"Two hundred and fifty dollars."

"It was a bargain at that price?"

"Certainly. It was a camera that would cost five hundred dollars in this country."

"Did you declare that camera in Customs when you brought it in here with you?"

"I didn't have to declare it. It had been used."

"Did you declare the camera when you came through Customs?"

"No."

"Did they ask you what you had bought in Mexico?"

"Yes."

"And you told them nothing?"

"Well . . . I didn't."

"You didn't? Who did?"

"Mr. Marshall."

"So you were staying in Mexicali and Mr. Marshall went across to bring you over here this morning?"

"Yes."

"And he told the Customs authorities in your presence that you had bought nothing while you were in Mexico?"

"Yes."

"Did you tell him any different? Did you interrupt to tell the Customs you had bought a camera?"

"No."

"And where did you get the money with which you purchased this camera?"

"That was from my winnings on the horse races."

"Oh, you won on the horse races."

"I won very substantially."

"How much?"

"I can't state, offhand."

"A hundred dollars?"

"More than that."

"Two hundred dollars?"

"More than that."

"Five hundred dollars?"

"More than that."

"You realize you are going to have to make a declaration of those winnings to the Collector of Internal Revenue and pay income taxes on them?"

"No. This money was won in a foreign country."

"That doesn't make any difference," Mason said. "You won the money and you brought it over to this country with you. Where is that money now?"

"It's . . . it's here and there."

"What do you mean, here and there?"

"Well, I have some of it with me."

"In your wallet at the present time?"

"Yes."

"Suppose we count it," Mason said, "and see just how much you won."

"That's none of your business, how much I have," Latty shouted. "It's my money."

"I think defense counsel is entitled to find out where this money came from," Judge Manly said, "and whether the prosecutor gave you funds with which to attend the races."

"He told me to have a good time and look around and enjoy myself."

"And gave you money for that purpose?"

"Well, he didn't tie any strings on it. He just said I'd need some money."

Judge Manly said, "Gentlemen, it's past the hour of noon and the Court is going to take a two-hour recess. Court will reconvene at two o'clock."

"May I ask one question?" Mason asked.

"Please be brief."

"What horses did you win on?"

"Well, there was— There were several horses."

"Name one. Where did you make your biggest winnings?"

"Well, there was a horse named Easter Bonnet."

"You won enough money on that horse to buy your camera?"

"Yes."

Judge Manly said, "Gentlemen, it is now fifteen minutes past the noon hour. The Court dislikes to interrupt this cross-examination but it's quite apparent we can't complete it within the next few minutes and therefore Court will take a recess until two o'clock this afternoon."

Judge Manly left the bench. Linda Calhoun hurried up the aisle to speak to George Latty, but before she could get there Marshall took Latty's arm and hurried him through the side door leading to the judge's chambers, leaving Linda standing there perplexed and embarrassed.

One of the newspaper photographers shot a picture of her as she stood there.

Mason turned hurriedly to Lorraine Elmore.

"Quick!" he said. "Tell me, is his testimony true? Were you sitting on the bed? Did you discuss your telephone call to Linda?"

Lorraine Elmore tearfully nodded.

"Then did you come back with Dewitt to the cabin?"

"Mr. Mason, as God is my judge, I am telling you the truth. I— How *could* I have got back? My car was stuck in the sand."

"Anything else you talked about at that time?" Mason asked.

As she was searching her recollection, Mason noticed Duncan Crowder, who had moved protectively to Linda Calhoun's side and was doing his best to cover her embarrassment and humiliation.

"I said something about the money. I remember that."

"What about it?"

"Well, when he wanted to go for a ride and— Well, I didn't think much of taking such a large sum of money in cash out in an automobile at night and I felt it would be dangerous. He laughed at me but I insisted that we should leave our money in the motel, that I was going to hide it. He laughed at me and said there wouldn't be any place to hide it where a person wouldn't look. I told him I was going to put it under the cushion of the overstuffed chair. I said that no one was apt to look in the unit of a motel, particularly when we were supposed to be sleeping there, but it was very easy to be held up in an automobile."

"And what did he say?"

"Well, he thought things over and finally agreed with me."

"Anything else you talked about at that time?" Mason asked.

"Not that I can remember."

"But you think Latty is telling the truth? You think he—".

"Yes, oh, yes! Oh, Mr. Mason, I'm so humiliated, so ashamed! I feel I could sink right through that floor. I just try to sit there and keep my eyes closed."

"All right," Mason said, "you're going to have to remain in custody during the noon hour."

She nodded tearfully, said, "But, Mr. Mason, Montrose *couldn't* have gone back there! I saw him killed! I tell you, I saw him with my own eyes!"

Mason said, "The question of the drugs hasn't come into it as yet, Mrs. Elmore, but I think you're going to have to recognize the strong possibility that you *may* have an erroneous recollection as to what happened. However, we're going to check every possible angle of the case. Just don't worry. We've got detectives on the job and we aren't done with George Latty yet."

"That man!" she said contemptuously. "What in the world can Linda see in a man of that sort?"

"I don't know," Mason admitted. "Personally, I think the judge is thoroughly disgusted with him, but of course his factual testimony is something that we're going to have to overcome in some way, either by evidence or by some other means. However, don't worry about it. I'll see you at two o'clock."

## Chapter 15

Lunching at a Mexican-style restaurant where they were able to get a small private dining room, Paul Drake filled Perry Mason in on details which he had picked up while court had been in session.

"We've been making like income tax agents," Drake said, "snooping around, finding every place the guy has been, backtracking him on his purchases. To date we can prove that he spent eight hundred and sixty-two dollars and seventy-five cents. But I can tell you something else, this guy Marshall is all set to file suit against you for defamation of character if you so much as intimate there was any question of bribery."

"Let him file," Mason said. "I'll intimate and be damned to him! I'll go even further than that. When a man pays the expenses of a witness while he's living in concealment, that's one thing. When he gives him a flat sum of money and tells him to pay his expenses out of that, that's something else.

"This guy, Marshall, is an eager beaver, a go-getter, but he's relatively inexperienced. There's a lot he has to learn about prosecuting murder cases."

"He's the darling of the county, however," Drake said dryly. "The guy is unmarried, an eligible bachelor, a smart cooky, and everybody's pulling for him.

"You're in a position where your reputation is assured. You can loose a case and it won't hurt, but if this guy wins a case against the great Perry Mason, it's going to make the whole community look good."

"I know," Mason said. "He's clever in the field of public

194

relations. He's used his newspaper friends to get that sort of a background and atmosphere."

"What are you going to do?" Drake asked.

"I don't know," Mason said, "but I'm going to go in there fighting and I'm going to stay in there fighting."

"And come out on top," Della Street said.

"Look at the thing from a reasonable basis," Mason said. "A woman like Lorraine Elmore, somewhat frustrated perhaps, nervous, but eminently respectable, isn't going to come all the way across the continent, pick up with someone and then murder him for fifteen thousand dollars or whatever it was he was carrying with him. That woman has means of her own and—"

"And that's not the motive he's going to try to prove," Drake interrupted.

"What isn't?"

"Money."

"What is?"

"Jealousy, disillusionment, frustrated rage."

"Go on," Mason said.

"I picked up something this morning that I've been thinking over," Drake said, "and I guess I have the answer. It occurred to me just now. I should have thought of it sooner."

"What is it?"

"This Belle Freeman."

"What about her?"

"She put through a long distance call to the Palm Court Motel. She asked to talk with Lorraine Elmore. Apparently the call was completed. She told Lorraine things about her boy friend, and Lorraine, in a fit of jealous rage, doped him and then stabbed him with an ice pick."

"How do you know about Belle Freeman?" Mason asked, his eyes narrowing.

"The manager told me that there was a long distance call for Lorraine Elmore from Los Angeles."

"That probably was Linda Calhoun calling."

"That's what I thought at first," Drake said, "but apparently this was another call."

Mason said, "I know the D.A. has Belle Freeman under subpoena. He caught her in this county and served a subpoena on her. Her boy friend lives here. I've been wondering what he intended to prove by her."

Mason was silently thoughtful for nearly a minute, then he said, "Find out about that horse, Easter Bonnet, Paul. See how much he actually paid off.

"The key figures in this case break out in a rash of gambling. Look at Howland Brent. He dashes to Las Vegas and starts plunging. He wins and quits. Then George Latty gets a little money and makes a beeline for the race track."

"But he didn't go to the race track," Drake said. "He must have placed the bets with a bookie somewhere."

"You haven't been able to get the bookie?" Mason asked.

Drake shook his head. "That's one of the things that puzzles me. We had been tailing Latty all the time but of course when he's inside a house talking with someone, you can't just barge in there and have a man listen to the conversation."

"No," Mason said thoughtfully, "but you *can* have a man go in there afterwards and find out what happened. Don't you have any idea where the bookie was?"

"We can make a good guess as to where he had to be, and that is in the curio shop, or the camera shop. Latty was in both places for a while."

"He may have bought some of that stuff as a stall to cover up the fact that he was plunging on the horses," Mason said. "Of course, he was in a good position to take a chance. He had a hundred and fifty dollars for expense money. He could plunge with that and if he won he had something to work with. If he lost, he could always ring up his friend, the district attorney, and say, 'I've been rolled and I have to have more money quick; otherwise I'll have to get in touch with Linda or Perry Mason.' "

"I wonder if he didn't do just that," Drake said, "I wonder if he didn't put the bite on Marshall. There's something weird about this thing."

"What about Brent?" Mason asked.

"Oh, it's the same old story—those thin walls again. Brent evidently had the idea that Lorraine was going to marry and from that time on her husband would be managing her affairs and there wouldn't be any room for him. So he was naturally concerned. It seems that the Elmore account was rather substantial and represented a fair source of income to Brent, so he did a little eavesdropping.

"Apparently he heard Lorraine tell you the story about her experiences, and Marshall is going to try to get his testimony in."

"That's a confidential communication to an attorney, isn't it?" Della Street asked.

"It depends," Mason said. "It's privileged as far as I'm concerned and as far as the client is concerned, but if some person happens to eavesdrop, that's another question, and probably a rather technical question. I'll have to argue the legal point. If it becomes important we'll ask for a twenty-four-hour continuance so we can dig into the authorities and see what the decisions hold."

"Is it a close point?" Drake asked.

"We'll make it a close point," Mason said.

Drake said, "Let me do a little telephoning. I want to find out about that horse."

Drake went to the telephone and was gone for some fifteen minutes. When he returned he cocked a quizzical eyebrow at Perry Mason.

"News?" Mason asked.

"News," Drake said.

"Shoot."

"The horse didn't win—he lost."

Slowly a grin spread over Mason's face. "What do you know," he said.

"*You* seem to know something," Della Street said.

Mason said, "I know a lot and I'm beginning to get the picture now."

The lawyer was silent for several minutes.

Paul Drake started to say something, but Della Street, with a finger on her lips, gestured him to silence.

Abruptly Mason pushed back his chair from the table, smiled, and slowly the smile broadened into a grin.

"Let's go on up to court and let Marshall pick up his little round pebble out of the stream bed."

"What do you mean, his pebble?" Drake asked.

"David and Goliath," Mason said. "It's about time for Marshall to start putting his pebble in the sling and whirling it around and around his head. He might even make himself dizzy."

# Chapter 16

Promptly at two o'clock Judge Manly took the bench, said, "Court is now in session. We will resume the hearing of the case of the People of the State of California versus Lorraine Elmore. Mr. Latty was on the stand. Come forward, Mr. Latty."

Latty resumed his position on the stand, and Judge Manly nodded to Perry Mason.

Mason said, "How much money have you actually spent since the fourth of this month, Mr. Latty?"

"I don't know."

"Can you approximate it?"

"No."

"Over a thousand dollars?"

"I don't think so."

"Don't you know?"

"No."

"All right, I'll go at it another way," Mason said. "How much money have you taken in since the fourth of the month?"

"Well, I had some money from Mr. Marshall for expenses."

"How much?"

"I believe around three hundred dollars in all."

"And many of your expenses you charged at the hotel in Mexicali?"

"Yes."

"Now, I'm not asking you about the things that you charged with the understanding that the county would pay for them later on, I'm asking you about how much actual cash you have received. You should know that."

"Well, let's see. I had about three hundred dollars from Mr. Marshall and— Well, that's about all, I guess."

"You had some money in your pocket when you went across the border at Tijuana? Money left from the twenty dollars I had given you and the twenty dollars given you by Linda Calhoun?"

"No, I was about broke at that time. I had to pay for the automobile I had rented, and with my necessary expenses I actually had to borrow money."

"Oh, you *borrowed* money," Mason said. "And who did you borrow that from?"

"Mr. Marshall."

"I see. Any other source of income?"

"No."

"Aren't you forgetting about your gambling?"

"Oh, yes, I made money from the horse races."

"How much?"

"I don't know. I would win the money and put it in my pocket and then bet and pay out the losses, but pocket the winnings."

"You didn't do this at the race track?"

"Well . . . I'm not sure."

Mason said, "You're sure whether you went to the race track or not. Now, did you bet at the race track or did you place your bets through a bookie?"

"I placed my bets through a bookie."

"And you have no idea how much money you won?"

"No. It was a fairly good-sized amount."

"More than a hundred dollars?"

"Oh, yes."

"More than five hundred?"

"It might have been."

"More than a thousand?"

"No. I wouldn't think it would be that much."

"You wouldn't *think* it would be that much."

"No."

"More than two thousand?"

"No, I know it wasn't more than two thousand."

"And what did you do with that money?"

"A good deal of it I spent."

"But you haven't spent it all?"

The witness hesitated. "I have a little."

"You're planning to leave for Boston as soon as your testimony is completed here?"

"Yes, as soon as I'm excused I'm taking a plane back to Boston."

"You have your ticket?"

"Yes."

"Now, how did you purchase your ticket when you came out?"

"With cash."

"You received the cash from what source?"

"Linda wired it to me."

"You got a single ticket or a round-trip ticket?"

"Oh, Your Honor," Marshall said, "this is the vice of going into all of this extraneous stuff. It seems to be completely interminable, and it makes no difference one way or another."

"Are you objecting?" Judge Manly asked.

"Yes, Your Honor."

"Overruled," Judge Manly said.

"Will you answer the question, please?" Mason said. "Did you have a round-trip ticket?"

"No, a one-way ticket."

"And do you now have a ticket on an eastbound plane, or just a reservation?"

"I . . . I have a ticket."

"The plane leaves at what time?"

"At eleven-thirty tonight."

"From Los Angeles?"

"From San Diego."

"And that ticket has been paid for?"

"Yes."

"Who paid for it?"

"Mr. Marshall made arrangements."

"In other words, he paid for it?"

"Yes."

"So, not only has the district attorney of this county started loaning you money as soon as he found out that you might be persuaded to give favorable testimony, but he has been trying to keep you in isolation so that you wouldn't disclose what your testimony was going to be and now he wants to get you out of the jurisdiction of the court as rapidly as possible."

"Your Honor, I object to that. I assign it as misconduct and I characterize the insinuation as a falsehood," Marshall said.

"Well," Judge Manly said, "I think I'll sustain that objection. After all, the Court will draw its own conclusions. I don't think there's anything in the testimony *as yet* to justify this charge.

"However, the Court will state that it is very much interested in the peculiar financial status of this witness. He seems to have been getting money from somewhere."

"From the horse races," Marshall said angrily. "He has been frank with the Court on that."

"He seems to have been unusually fortunate," Judge Manly said.

"That also can happen," Marshall pointed out.

"Doubtless it has happened," Judge Manly said.

Mason said, "But your big winning was from this horse, Easter Bonnet?"

"Yes," Latty said.

"You don't remember how much you won?"

"It was rather a large amount."

"And you're sure you won it on that horse?"

Mason stood looking at the witness for a moment, then suddenly said, "George, why don't you tell the truth? You didn't win that money in a horse race. That horse lost."

"Lost!" Latty said.

"Lost," Mason said. "Now tell us the truth. Where did you get that money?"

"I . . . I—"

Mason said, "You could hear the conversation in the adjoining unit there at the Palm Court Motel very plainly."

"Yes."

"And in that same conversation that you overheard, the parties were discussing what they were going to do with their cash. Mrs. Elmore didn't want to take the money in the form of cold, hard cash with them when they went on that ride. She had something like thirty-five thousand dollars, and Dewitt had something like fifteen thousand dollars, all in cash. They discussed where they would hide it. That was part of that same conversation that you were listening to."

"I . . . I didn't hear all of it."

"You heard enough of it to know that they were concealing the money under the cushions of the overstuffed chair. Now, I submit to you, young man, that you tried to follow them, lost their trail, came back, started experimenting with the door which led through to the Unit fourteen which Montrose Dewitt was occupying, found that you could open that door by turning the bolt on your side, entered that unit and looked in the chair and found some fifty thousand dollars in cash. You had never had any money. You had been dependent upon friends for money. You have been placed in the embarrassing and humiliating position of having to ask your fiancée for money for every little thing you did. You couldn't resist that temptation. You took that money."

"Oh, Your Honor," Marshall said, "that is absolutely absurd. There is no foundation for such a charge. This is not a question. It is an accusation. It is objected to as being not proper cross-examination."

"Overruled," Judge Manly snapped. "Now, young man, *I* want you to answer that question and I want a straightforward answer. Remember, you're under oath."

"I did nothing of the sort," Latty said indignantly.

"All right," Mason said, "where's your baggage? You're all packed up to leave here and go to San Diego just as soon as you finish testifying. Where's your baggage?"

"In the district attorney's office."

"Would you have any objection to having that baggage brought here and having it opened?"

"Certainly I would! I see no reason to subject my personal baggage to an examination by anyone."

"Is there anything in there that you're trying to conceal?"

"No."

"All right," Mason said, walking two paces toward the red-faced witness. "I'm going to look inside that baggage. I'm going to get a search warrant if I have to. Now, you're under oath. Remember that baggage is going to be searched. Is there or is there not money in it?"

"Of course there's money in it. I told you I won some money."

"Is there as much as twenty thousand dollars in that baggage?"

"I . . . I don't know how much I won."

"You don't know whether you won as much as twenty thousand dollars?"

"No."

"Is there thirty thousand dollars in there?"

"I tell you, I don't know."

"All right," Mason said, "I'm going to give you one more chance to tell the truth, and remember, you're under oath. Did you go into Dewitt's motel unit? Now, before you answer that question, remember that the police have testified there were some fingerprints in that room they couldn't identify but which were sufficiently definite to—"

"All right, I went in there," Latty said. "It's just as you thought. After I found I had lost them, I came back and started fooling with that connecting door and I found I could turn the bolt on my side and open the door. I found that the person on the other side hadn't turned the bolt to the position which locked the door on that side. So, by turning the knob which opened the bolt on my side, I could go in. I went in and looked around."

"And found that money," Mason said.

The witness hesitated for a long, uncomfortable moment.

Marshall got to his feet to make an objection, and Judge Manly motioned him to sit down.

Latty suddenly lowered his head. "All right," he said. "I got the money."

"I thought so," Mason said. "Now, did you kill Montrose Dewitt?"

The witness raised tear-filled eyes. "I swear to you, Mr. Mason, I swear absolutely I know nothing about that. I did not kill him. The temptation as far as the money was concerned was too much. I intended first to take it and then get in the good graces of Lorraine Elmore by returning her money to her at the proper time. I felt that Montrose Dewitt was a confidence man and a potential murderer and I didn't know whether I'd ever return his part of the money. But I didn't kill him."

Mason turned, walked back to his chair at the counsel table, seated himself and said, "No further questions."

Marshall stood looking first at the tearful witness, then at the stern face of the judge. He turned, walked over to the counsel table, whispered to his assistant, then said, "Your Honor, this testimony naturally comes as a great surprise to me. . . . I . . . I'm going to ask the court for a continuance."

"You can't have one unless the defense attorney stipulates to it," Judge Manly said. "This hearing is supposed to be concluded at one sitting unless the defendant joins in a motion for a continuance. . . . Now then, I'm going to ask you, what do you intend to do about this witness?"

"I . . . I repudiate him."

"I'm not talking about repudiating him. Here's a man who has been committing perjury and has just admitted to grand theft. What are you going to do about it?"

"I . . . I can appreciate the temptation but I suppose I will have to have him held."

"I would certainly think so," Judge Manly said.

He turned to Mason. "What is the position of the defense in regard to a continuance?"

Mason said, "I have no desire to take advantage of the prosecution's surprise, if the Court please. I am willing to

205

consent to a continuance. I may state, however, that Mr. Latty had not been concealed as far as we were concerned. We have had investigators keeping him in sight, knew where he was, and knew that he was spending a great deal of money.

"Under the circumstances, and knowing that he was entirely without funds when he had gone over into Mexico, it was only natural that I became interested in the source of his funds. At first I had formed the perfectly natural conclusion that this money must have been supplied by the person who was trying to keep him concealed. I am sorry I charged the prosecutor with seeking to bribe this witness."

"The prosecutor has only himself to blame," Judge Manly said.

Marshall, considerably chastened, said, "I regret this entire situation. May we ask for an adjournment until tomorrow morning at ten o'clock?"

"Satisfactory to the defendant," Mason said, "but I would suggest that the defendant be released on her own recognizance until the hearing tomorrow."

"I object to that," Marshall said.

"Then I think we will object to the continuance," Mason said.

"May I have a fifteen-minute recess to discuss the matter with my assistant?" Marshall asked.

"That would seem to be a very reasonable request," Judge Manly said. "Court will take a fifteen-minute recess. And as far as this witness, Latty, is concerned, I want him taken into custody. The Court is not satisfied in the least with the explanation of his conduct that has been made. If he went into that room, if he took that money, then I see no reason why he couldn't have used the murder weapon as well."

"Then how did it get in the defendant's car?" Marshall asked.

"It got there because it was put there," Judge Manly said. "This witness was out a second time and that was after he had secured the money. How do we know where he went? We only have his statement for it."

"I didn't kill him! I tell you, I didn't!" Latty protested.

Judge Manly said, "You've told us a lot of things, young man. The Court is going to insist that you be taken into custody. The Court is going to order you into custody for perjury and for grand larceny. Now then, Court will take a fifteen-minute recess."

As Judge Manly left the bench, Lorraine Elmore squeezed Mason's arm until he could feel the tips of her fingers biting into the flesh. "Oh, Mr. Mason!" she said. "Oh, Mr. Mason!"

Linda Calhoun came hurrying forward. Her first objective was George Latty, but Latty, seeing her coming, hurried toward the exit door through which prisoners were taken from the courtroom and a deputy sheriff hurrying after him, said, "Just a minute, Latty. You're in custody."

Linda swerved over toward the defense group.

"Oh, Duncan," she said, "I feel so perfectly, utterly, absolutely terrible!"

"About what?"

"That heel," she said. "I made all sorts of sacrifices to keep him in law school and I *knew* how Aunt Lorraine felt about him. I . . ."

She blinked back tears.

Lorraine Elmore embraced her, said, "There, there, darling. It's all right. *Everything's* going to be all right now."

Newspaper reporters crowded around, asking for a story. Flash bulbs popped.

Mason said, "I'm sorry, gentlemen. We only have fifteen minutes and we have to confer on some strategy. With your permission we're going to move over here to a corner of the courtroom."

Mason beckoned to the others and they huddled in a deserted corner of the courtroom back of the judge's bench.

"Okay, what happens now?" Drake asked.

"Now," Mason said, "we begin to get the picture."

"You mean that Latty killed him?"

207

"Gosh, no," Mason said. "Latty didn't kill him. Latty hasn't the guts. He hasn't the initiative. He hasn't the determination. He's a jackal, not a lion."

"All right, what did happen?" Drake asked.

Mason said, "Dewitt had to have an accomplice."

"What do you mean, an accomplice?"

"It's plain as day," Mason said. "He wanted to disappear. He had two entities, two separate identities. One was Montrose Dewitt, the other was Weston Hale.

"Weston Hale worked in a financial institution where he had an opportunity to handle a good many sums of money. I have an idea that the identity of Dewitt was taken for the purpose of enabling Hale to embezzle money and vanish without leaving any trace, but something happened to change the plans, and Hale was left with this alter ego of Dewitt on his hands.

"He found that by using this identity, he could victimize women and pick up quite a little money on the side.

"Now then, something happened to the Dewitt personality and Hale decided to kill off Dewitt, to get rid of the character, and he decided to do it under such circumstances that it would not only be profitable for him but so he would completely clean the slate.

"So he planned to let it appear he had been murdered. However, he wanted to do more than disappear. He wanted to take Lorraine's thirty-five thousand dollars with him.

"So he went out in the car with her to a predetermined destination and there his accomplice held up the car."

"But how do you account for the terrific beating he took?" Lorraine Elmore asked tearfully. "I saw it. I heard it."

"That's the point," Mason said. "That's part of the game. He was beaten up with a rolled-up newspaper painted black so it looked like a club. The impact of the blows was terrific but had no more real force behind them than a good lick with a fly swatter."

"And then what happened?" Drake asked.

"Then everything went according to plan for a while,"

Mason said. "The accomplice drove behind you, Mrs. Elmore, until you got stuck in the sand. Then he turned around, went back and picked up Dewitt, or Hale, and returned to the motor court. That's when they intended to get the money and leave. And then something happened."

"Such as what?" Drake asked.

"Such as the fact that the accomplice decided since Hale or Dewitt had been officially murdered and his murder was going to be reported to the police, it might be just as well to let Dewitt actually become a corpse, and the accomplice skip out with fifty thousand dollars."

"But Latty has the fifty thousand," Drake said.

"That was a fluke. They hadn't counted on Latty," Mason said.

"Well, then—who was the accomplice?" Drake asked.

"Someone Dewitt was close to, someone he had done business with . . ."

"You mean Belle Freeman?" Linda asked incredulously.

The door from chambers opened, and Judge Manly entered the courtroom. Everyone hurriedly took their places.

Judge Manly said to Marshall, "Has the prosecutor's office agreed on whether it wishes a continuance on condition that the defendant be released on her own recognizance?"

"If the Court please, we simply can't consent to that," Marshall said. "We would very much like a continuance but we can't consent to the release of the defendant on her own recognizance."

"Well, I can appreciate the defendant's position," Judge Manly said. "Simply because the prosecution has been surprised by a very peculiar development in this case and desires time to meet the situation, is no reason why the defendant should stay in custody for another twenty-four hours. If you aren't prepared to make that stipulation, proceed with your case."

Mason said, "Perhaps, Your Honor, if I could ask two or three more questions of one witness, we might clear up the case to such an extent an adjournment wouldn't be necessary."

"What witness?" Judge Manly asked.

"One who can tell us something about Montrose Dewitt we may have overlooked," Mason said. "Ronley Andover."

Judge Manly glanced at the prosecutor.

"I certainly have no objections," Marshall said.

Judge Manly nodded to Andover. "You will resume your position on the witness stand, Mr. Andover. You have already been sworn."

Andover took his place on the witness stand, his manner indicating puzzled surprise.

Mason approached Andover, watching the man's eyes as he advanced.

"Mr. Andover," he said, "on the night of the third, where were you?"

"In Los Angeles. You know that. I was in bed with the flu."

"Did you leave Los Angeles at any time during the night?"

"Certainly not."

"Then," Mason said, "how did it happen that your fingerprint was one of the unidentified fingerprints found in the Palm Court motel in Calexico?"

Andover stiffened with apprehension. "It wasn't. It couldn't have been."

Mason turned to the sheriff. "Sheriff, I'd like to have you take this man's fingerprints," he said.

The sheriff looked at Marshall.

"We object," Marshall said. "We feel that this is an attempt to intimidate the witness."

"Ordinarily I would rule with you," Judge Manly said. "But in this case, Mr. Prosecutor, there have been too many bizarre developments, and counsel for the defense has been able to call the turn so far. Let's have this man's fingerprints taken."

"Now, wait a minute!" Andover shouted. "You have no right to do that! I'm subpoenaed here as a witness. I'm not under arrest. I'm not under suspicion of anything."

"Any objection to giving your fingerprints?" Mason asked.

"I don't have to."

"Any objection?" Mason asked.

"Yes!" Andover shouted.

"All right," Mason said, "what's the objection?"

Andover, looking like a trapped animal, suddenly jumped up from the witness stand. "I'm not going to stay here and be subjected to any abuse of this sort. I know my rights."

"Now, just a minute," Judge Manly said. "Sheriff, take that man into custody if he tries to leave here. Under the circumstances it would seem that this matter of the fingerprints may be of tremendous importance."

Andover suddenly lashed out at the sheriff, turned and started running from the courtroom.

The sheriff shouted, "You're under arrest! Halt or I'll shoot!"

Andover slammed the exit door in the sheriff's face.

The sheriff wrenched it open, pulling out his gun as he did so.

The courtroom went into an uproar as spectators struggled to get to the exit doors in order to see what was happening.

Mason glanced up at the bench and caught Judge Manly's eye.

"And now," Judge Manly said, "the Court will continue the case of its own motion, and of its own motion will order the defendant released on her own recognizance, unless the prosecutor wants to dismiss the case."

Marshall hesitated for a moment, then threw out his hands in a gesture of surrender.

"Very well," he said, "the case is dismissed." And without a word, either to the defendant or Perry Mason, stalked from the courtroom.

## Chapter 17

Mason, Della Street, Duncan Crowder, Linda Calhoun, Lorraine Elmore and Paul Drake gathered in Duncan Crowder's office.

"Well," Crowder said, "I guess the local David with his slingshot made a clean miss, and Goliath Mason is still with us."

Mason said, "Thanks to some darned good local assistance."

Crowder bowed.

Drake said, "Let's see if I get this straight, Perry. Andover was to be the accomplice. He went to the place that had previously been picked out for the holdup and where Dewitt had arranged to have Lorraine Elmore. He put a gun on Dewitt, ordered him out of the car, took him back a ways, beat him up with a newspaper rolled up and painted black to resemble a club; then came back, forced Mrs. Elmore to drive to a point where she would be stuck in the sand; then went back, picked up Dewitt and they returned to the motel, apparently intending to stay just long enough to pick up the money and leave."

"That was the idea," Mason said, "but when he was searching the car, Andover found that big bottle of barbiturates in the glove compartment. That gave him an idea. He hastily dumped the capsules into a whiskey bottle, waited until they had dissolved, gave Dewitt a drink in the dark, and by the time they arrived at the motel Dewitt was so groggy he hardly knew what was going on.

"In all probability he actually went to sleep almost as soon as they reached the cabin, and then just in order to make certain he wouldn't have any more trouble with

Dewitt, and knowing that he had a perfect pigeon, Andover simply got rid of Dewitt by using an ice pick. Then he detoured back to the place where the stalled automobile had been left. He didn't take the road that Lorraine had taken, however; he went out on the Holtville road and drove south until he came to the sand patch. Then he put the ice pick in Lorraine's car and left a capsule on the front seat. By that time Lorraine Elmore was walking back toward the highway.

"Having done that job, Andover went back to Los Angeles, used an extract of onion or some other material to which he was allergic to start his nose and his eyes running, went to bed and pretended he was incapacitated with the flu.

"But the amateur criminal invariably overlooks some one important point. He forgot about leaving his fingerprints in the motel, and when he realized that he had done so he realized that the slip was disastrous—something he could never explain."

"But why did he tear up Lorraine Elmore's unit?" Drake asked. "Oh, wait a minute—I see. He thought the money was in the overstuffed chair in Dewitt's unit. When he looked for it there and didn't find it, he thought then it must have been in Lorraine's unit so he went in there and ransacked that."

Mason nodded. "He had the key," he said. "Remember he took everything from Lorraine, including her handbag. Incidentally that was a tip-off—that the handbag was found in the motel unit.

"At the time the holdup was planned, Dewitt had no way of knowing that Lorraine would insist on leaving the money in the motel. He naturally thought she would take it with her, but when he suggested the midnight ride in order to talk things over—which was, of course, all part of the plan which had previously been worked out with Andover—Lorraine insisted on hiding the money in the motel.

"At the time that didn't seem to make any difference, because Dewitt and Andover could take the money from the motel just as easily as they could take it from Lorraine."

Della said, "But what gets me, Perry, is how you figured it out. How did you know that the accomplice was Andover?"

"It was very, very simple," Mason said. "It was a point that I completely overlooked at the moment, and it's going to be a long time before I forgive myself for it."

"What do you mean?"

"As soon as I realized what had happened," Mason said, "that is, what must have happened, I knew that Dewitt must have had an accomplice."

Della Street nodded.

"So I started turning over in my mind the possibilities and wondering who that accomplice could have been," Mason said. "Then it suddenly became perfectly apparent. It had to be Andover."

"Why?"

"Because," Mason said, "Andover got the fifteen thousand dollars for Dewitt, the fifteen thousand dollars that was to be the bait he was using in order to get Lorraine to take her thirty-five thousand dollars in cash. He stood on the curb and handed the envelope containing the money to Dewitt when Lorraine drove the car to the place which Dewitt had designated for the meeting."

"Go on," Della Street said. "I still don't see it."

"Remember," Mason said, "that Andover had only known Dewitt as Weston Hale, according to his story. And he didn't know that Weston Hale had an artificial eye. Yet at the time Andover handed over the money, Hale was masquerading as Dewitt and had the black patch over his eye.

"If Andover had been on the square and had been telling the truth, the first thing he would have mentioned was that he was surprised when he saw his friend to see the black patch over his eye."

Drake snapped his fingers. "Hell, yes," he said.

"I guess that does it," Della Street said, "but I do wish somebody would explain to me what caused Howland

Brent to suddenly make a beeline for Las Vegas and start plunging."

"That," Mason said, "is puzzling."

There was a moment's silence. Then Lorraine Elmore said, "I am going to tell you the reason for that. I hope it won't go any further because I am satisfied Howland is thoroughly repentant and there is no danger of any future lapses.

"The fact of the matter is that Brent had some very urgent personal financial obligations. He had some money of his own coming in within a few weeks and knowing that I was out of town and had some funds which he could use, he dipped into my funds. Then, when he realized that I was about to get married, he knew that my husband would demand an accounting and his defalcation would be exposed.

"The man became absolutely desperate. He flew out here to try and see me. He wanted to confess, ask my forgiveness and arrange for a loan until he could make restitution.

"When he saw that I was being charged with murder, he realized that instead of getting out of the frying pan he had got into the fire. There was only one alternative as far as he was concerned. That was to stake everything on a last desperate gamble.

"So he decided to go to Las Vegas to plunge on the tables there. If he won the amount of his defalcations, he was going to quit and never gamble again as long as he lived. If he lost, he intended to commit suicide.

"I'm hoping that none of you will ever repeat this. I feel that you are entitled to an explanation. I am also certain that Howland Brent has learned his lesson and that he will never gamble again as long as he lives."

"So that explains it!" Drake said. "The guy certainly had me puzzled."

"Well," Crowder said, laughing, "all's well that ends well, and this case hasn't done me any harm. Thanks a lot for having me associated, Perry."

"Thanks to you," Mason said.

Drake said, "You sure gave Crowder the spotlight, Perry."

Mason turned to Drake. "Duncan told me there was a young woman in the courtroom whom he wanted to impress—"

Under Crowder's desk Della Street kicked Mason's shin so hard he winced with pain.

Linda Calhoun's face suddenly became a fiery red.

"Well, he certainly made a great impression on *me*," Della Street said, laughing.

The ringing of the telephone gave Crowder a chance to turn to the instrument and to some extent recover his composure.

When he had finished the conversation, he turned to Mason and said, "That was the press. They want a picture of us all taken together here in my office. I guess it's all right, isn't it?"

Mason nodded. "Anything you want is okay, Duncan," he said, *"anything."*